Anthology o˙ from Novels and a Short Story - Edition 2025

Glimpses into the Literary Worlds of Ten Portsmouth Authors

Compiled by the Portsmouth Authors' Collective

The Portsmouth Authors Collective is a group of writers based in and around Portsmouth, UK, and was founded by Loree Westron. Their mission is to showcase the amazing work coming out of this corner of the world.

The individual authors of this anthology assert their copyright © 2025

Contents

Contents v

'Revolt of the Machines' by JS Adams 1
    Introduction 1
    Chapter Six 2
    About the author 22

'Inscription' by Fiona Ballard 23
    Introduction 23
    Chapter 1 Beatrice – 1999 24
    About the author 43

'Unjudging Love: The Enigma of Dylan Thomas' by Josh Brown 44
    Introduction 44
    From Chapter 4 Sailing Toward Death 45
    About the author 63

'Getting the Measure of Things' by Patsy Collins 66
    Introduction 66
    A short story 'Getting the Measure of Things' 66
    About the author 82

'Fallen Angels - Alchemy or Artifice' by Vicky Fox 83
    Introduction 83
    From Chapter 3 - Pitdown Hall 84
    About the author 108

'The Perfect Fool' by Nick Morrish 109
    Introduction 109
    Chapter 17 Firestarter 109
    About the author 131

'Kissed to Death' by Gillian Fernandez Morton 132
    Introduction 132
    Prologue 132
    About the author 148

'Sometimes When I Sleep' by Helen Salsbury 150
    Introduction 150
    Once 151
    About the author 177

'Mute' by Richard Salsbury 178
    Introduction 178
    Chapter 1 178
    Chapter 2 193
    About the author 203

'A Very Important Teapot' By Steve Sheppard 204
    Introduction 204
    Extract 205
    About the author 224

'Revolt of the Machines' by JS Adams

Introduction

It is the future. Despised desk clerk bureaucrat (Harvey Tannon) revels in his post, working for the detestable *Department of Tagging*.

Meanwhile his work colleagues are all gradually being replaced by Imitons, a caste of the various nano-morph machines, that now occupy nearly all corners of industry and leisure.

On the eve of the only Festival permitted, Tannons world is suddenly turned upside down by the beautiful and rebellious Jenny who costs him his job.

Jobless and destitute, Tannon awakens the day after, with the god of all hangovers, only to realise he maybe one of the very people left alive in London.

The Revolt of the Machines has begun...

Chapter Six
PRINCESS AND THE TOAD

I suppose you might call it my comeuppance, when on the very same day of *The Festival of Yana,* the young woman in black, visited upon me a third time. But this would not be on the gutter tube-trains as before. This time, she actually came into my office at the *Department of Revenue & Tagging*.

It had been a few weeks since I last saw her, but the moment she came in that squalid grey room, it was like all the filth and grime of the dank office melted away in her very presence.

From that moment on, I was hooked again by her bright hazel eyes and tumbling black hair, framed by a gothic black hood and cloak. She relented an air of cool intelligence. In another world she might have been a princess of great importance.

But if Terry was still here, he'd probably make some crude sexual gestures behind her by now. God I missed his stupid-ass jokes. Actually I missed all my old work colleagues. It suddenly occurred to me, that besides the woman in black, I was the only other human being in the office now. All the other staff were robots. *Imitons.* Useless bloody things.

She crossed the rows of them, seated at their desks but made no attempt to approach them for help. I regarded her curvy features. Even if I did go revelling tonight, it would be by myself. But as I sat there mulling at my screen (and pretending not to look at her), there was part of me that wondered how my evening might play out, if I could somehow strike up the nerve to ask this woman to join me for a drink.

On the other hand, I had to remind myself that a free spirited women of her apparent character, was hardly at a loss for the demanding attentions of competing admirers. Moreover, we lived worlds apart. Worlds that couldn't possibly ever intersect, on any level other than her breaching protocol and me reprimanding her, as I did with countless others.

But against all odds, perhaps fate had now come into play? For as she looked around the many desks with their many faceless robot workers, she (by some miracle), approached me instead.

She did not recognise me of course, clad head to foot in my mud-green water and spit-proof overalls, face mask and those ridiculous bulging eye goggles. What a pair we must make.

Like a scene from a fairy tale, now she faced me, the princess, while I festered in my dark corner, a green and wart-laden toad, upon my lily pad.

She sat in the seat and said nothing but produced a bundle of documents, pushing them before me, and so I examined them, trying to ignore her intriguing attire. Just black. Like velvet.
I ignored too the moment she flipped back the hood revealing that slender neck and long dark hair. My heart fluttered, skipped, danced, near fell down the stairs.

She sat stiffly, twiddling her perfect thumbs between her perfect fingers, devoid of any marital rings. She cleared her throat loudly. Then she spoke.

'I'm here...' She began. 'because my disabled mother's been blocked?' Her American accent was unmistakable. It was the same voice that narrated the disc. That perplexing disc she had inadvertently dropped on the subway that time. I was it on purpose? The disc I took home and watched. A disc full of outlandish crack-pot theories. Of rebellion against tyranny and so on. A disc I should have disposed of but for reason couldn't.

And now what luck. Here she was before me, a ringleader no doubt, vulnerable and unawares. I had her right in the palm of my hand, to do with what I pleased.

*

It was often difficult to separate my feelings from the job at hand. Certainly, when it came to her, my cold heart seemed to melt. I was a sucker for good-looking women and she obviously knew that, or she wouldn't have gone out of her way to invoke such a reaction. To dress in such a provocative manor that went against every sense of societal decency.

I imagine she was the type that attended those illicit gatherings (of more than six) and perhaps (dare I imagined), she even danced ! Gyrating in a vulgar fashion to inappropriate music, spreading her female pheromones and other ghastly disease-spreading odours, upon unsuspecting righteous citizens.

She was beautiful yes but judging by that disc, had to be part of some large rebellion network. Nobody else dared carry such items. Why I never turned the disc over to the proper authorities was by my own foolishness. But now she was in my office, that mistake could be easily be rectified. All I had to do was turn her in.

But again for some reason I hesitated. Before I knew it, I was suddenly talking about the festival to her. I couldn't remember what exactly I said. Something along the lines of *would she be attending it?* Or words to that effect. She tilted her head to one side, before brushing her fingers through her long dark hair and then she laughed.

'The Festival?' She snubbed, holding nothing back. 'Are you for real? What do I look like to you? Some friken *Jersey Queen*?' She gritted her teeth with contempt and began to rant about how the festival was nothing more than a sham, an excuse to rape and pillage and get away with murder, under the guise of legalised alcohol. I sat taken back, a little shocked by her.

For she looked like a *princess*, yet spoke like the worst of the *Old Jersey Queen guttersnipes*. I shuffled my papers nervously. Eventually she calmed and came down to the heart of the matter. 'I'm sorry.' She sighed. 'I'm ranting. It's just that my sister... she was at one a few years ago. She was...'

There was a pause as she bowed her head and fumbled with her shoulder bag.

'You were saying Miss?'

'Look, about my mother?' She said coldly. 'She was blocked and I don't even know why. We've been trying to get through to somebody now for nearly three weeks!'

'Three weeks?' I said jovially. 'Some people have to wait three months! What's your secret? Don't tell me, I think I know!' I sniggered. But she return the sentiment. Uh-oh.

'What?' She said. Suddenly she got to her feet and leant across the desk, holding me point blank to her steely gaze.

'Now Listen Here!' She said, her voice getting louder. *'You Little Friken ...Frog!'*

All heads turned towards us. The faceless Imitons stopped and regarded her. Now she was in full rant mode.

'I've been trying to get through to your friken department for three friken weeks! And all I get is the friken run-around! I've been put on hold or cut off or told to ring back later. So now I've had to come all the way down here!'

'Wait. I'm sorry. You mean to say you don't have an actual appointment then?'

'No! I don't!'

'I'm sorry I can't see you without an actual appointment.'

'For Godssakes! I can't get a friken appointment! Nobody answers the friken phones! All I get is put on hold by some pencil pushing frog *like you!!*'

By now I was somewhat shaken. How dare she talk to a *Revenue Tag Inspector* in such a manor! I should have blocked her ass right there and then or left her to the mercy of my Imiton co-workers, but oh god. Those legs. Those long, long legs. And that heaving chest. My heart suddenly began to flutter. It was a strange sensation, like a hamster having a heart attack.

By now four Imiton security guards had approached, their hands poised on belted truncheons, ready to draw them at the first sign of physical violence.

Sensing their presence the woman began to cower. The Imitons flanked her, truncheons poised. I quickly raised my hand to stop them. She in turn, nervously smiled back at them, her lips trembling, from one expression to another. Surrounded by the faceless guards, she sat back down. I nodded for the them to leave, to which they receded back into their alcoves. Regaining composure, she continued.

'*Look.*' She sighed '*All I want to know is why my mother was blocked ok?*'

She went onto explain how her poor elderly wheelchair-bound mother couldn't leave the house or do any online shopping etc because her tag was blocked and blah-blah-blah.

But I wasn't really taking any of this in. Perhaps I was in love but the evil frog within reminded me of the power I now had over her, to crush her into nothing!

*

By now she was red faced and quickly reached into her shoulder bag. I half-expected a gun perhaps and warned her to keep her hands where I could see them.

'chill out' She sighed, producing a small portable fan to cool herself with, fluttering it about her exposed shoulders and neck.

Everything about her was of another time. *'Chill-out'.* I hadn't heard that expression in years. It was considered *Dads Talk.* Up there with words like: *Groovy, Sick* and *Cool.* Bygone words of the old world. Even profanity was frowned upon these days. Swear words were often flagged (particularly with children), thus one might find themselves blocked for up to two weeks.

I spent many a time lecturing kids on how profanity created division between the social classes and led to dissidence. But if it was up to me, I'd have the little blighters blocked permanently.

Yet here I was with a fully grown woman, using such words as if she owned them body and soul. Breathing life into old redundancies and to hell with all the consequences. She looked away, coughed into her fist and apologised for her outburst.

'Look. Mr er..?'

'Tannon.' I said. 'But you can call me Harvey.'

'Mr Tannon. Let me be honest...' She then went onto explain that it was not the first time that her mother had been blocked and that it was becoming a frequent issue, as she became older and frail. Now the continual switching off of her mother's tag-implant was making life a misery.

She gave me the usual sob-story about how the block made the most basic things in her mother's life totally inaccessible. Just getting on a bus for example or paying for food or whatnot.

How her mother was always getting locked out of the house and if she wasn't there looking after her, her mother would be in a right old mess. The more she attempted to explain the more her voice suddenly began to rise again. I scrolled through my tortious-screen, trying to ignore her emotional meltdown and the more I stared at the screen, the more I felt my dependable toad-self returning again. I then found her mother's details regarding *'offspring'*.

Her mother did indeed have two daughters, Jenny and Amy. The latter had died. (deceased five years ago). Cause of Death: Suicide. It was all there in the report. One surviving daughter, from a messy divorce, the photos were older but undeniably her.

This impossible woman in black. The evil toad in me began to take over. Accessing her files, I learned she was an art student drop-out. And as I suspected a dissident. Part of the *Stop the Gunk Campaign* in fact, that her stupid disc had mentioned. Now the toad was on a roll.

Finally! I had a lead! Somebody on the inside of all this dissidence, my big break to promotion at last! And so I began to play with her with great delight. It would be so easy just to access her tag and block her just for the hell of it. Just switch off her chip and be done with her, maybe make her my pet and make her do tricks. I swung the monitor screen around so she couldn't see it.

'Hmm....oooh ...oh dear ....' I said staring at the screen as if it was really important. Rubbing my hands together, I relished in my little power games. Terry would have been proud. The more I said these *oohs* and *ahhs* and *hmms*, and stared at the screen, the more she began to squirm in her seat, looking increasingly concerned.

'What is it?' She said leaning forward and touching my desk.

'It says here that your mother didn't complete the online IRT form for the beginning of this financial year...' I swung the screen around to show her, to which she began to sigh impatiently, rubbing her face in dismay.

'What? No, no...' She began. 'No wait. That can't be! I returned that form for her last year and in plenty of time!' She sat back and folded her arms, her brown eyes darted at me and then back at the paper work, I suddenly felt something stirring within me again. Perhaps it was her zest for life. Perhaps it was her vibrant character. Whatever it was, it simply didn't matter. How could it? My heart was pure stone, or so I wanted to believe.

'Well I can't help you with that miss, sorry. The law states that she must submit any late IRT forms attached with the *'extenuating circumstances form'*, which it says here you did not enclose in her original application. I must also point out that you might be breaching fraud if you filled out these forms on her behalf without signing the P-37X/9 waver form...' Her eyes narrowed, glaring at me in utter contempt for what I represented.

'Sorry?'

'There's nothing I can do miss. Your mother needs to come down here and then we can process her claim.'

'But she's in a friken wheelchair you idiot! And she's been blocked? How the hell is she supposed to get down here on the bus, or even the trains? If she's friken blocked they won't let her onboard now will they!'

I suppose she had a point. But that wasn't my problem now was it? I resigned to the fact that it didn't really matter what I felt about this woman, she now absolutely despised me. She then tried to argue, that the former staff-member she dealt with at the time, didn't have a P-37X/9 waver form, nor did anyone mention that such a form even existed or that she was breaking any laws. She simply wasn't listening to reason. All she had to do was wheel her mother down here and it would all be sorted. What was her problem?

Losing her patience again, she got to her feet, hands on hips and demanded I do something about it all, as if I had a magic wand or something.

'Now miss, please there is no cause for that kind of language! I'm obliged to tell you that-' But she cut me off like a sword through my heart.

'Listen up you moron, I didn't come all the way down here to your stupid pathetic office just to deal with petty jobsworth cretins like you. What are you supposed to be anyway? You look like stupid frog in that dumb-ass get-up. You know what? You're no better than all this lot...' She motioned at the row of Imitons sat behind their desks. 'Look at them! Nothing but a bunch of stupid useless ...dummies!' The Imiton's turned to look at her, almost as if they were offended.

By now she was pretty much in tears and the more I tried to calm her down, the worse she became.

'*JUST TURN MY MOTHERS TAG BACK ON! NOW!*' She screamed, banging her hand again on the table in absolute fury. By now the Imitons were up from their desks. The security types left their alcoves once more and began to circle her, closing the gap. Exhausted, she slumped in the chair sobbing, her head in her hands, surrounded by four Imitons, who towered over her.

'Look...' She whimpered, covering her eyes in shame. 'My mother is very old. She doesn't understand all this.' She begged and pleaded with me but it simply came back to the same situation, that I could not process her claim without her mother being present.

In the end I realised there was nothing for it but to keep her mother blocked until a full investigation into this matter was resolved and warned her that if she did not calm down, I would have to block her as well. Tears suddenly became fire again.

'Look.' She said angrily. 'I have filled out all your stupid forms a dozen million friken times already, okay? I've been put on hold for weeks on end and if you dare mention what the law says one more friken time! I will spit in your friken face your friken goggle-eyed frog!'

At last! This was the moment I had been waiting for. It always came down to this. The spitting. Oh how I loved it when they spat at me! It was what I lived for, or rather I used to. If Terry was here, we would have done bets on how quickly we could work up a client before they lost all refrain and gobbed at us or tried to throw a table across the room. Not that they could anyway, since most of the furniture was bolted down, even the seats couldn't be lifted without being demagnetised.

But I digress. Unable throw stuff about the office, there was nothing left but to gob at us and we knew it. But Terry was gone. They were all gone. Now it was just me, making petty wagers with nobody...but myself.

Perhaps I had already become a machine, I didn't know anymore, however I pointed to the target painted on my rain mac and told her take to her best shot. It was always worth the pay check bonus If I could manipulate the client into *visceral abuse*.

It was of course the only way I could make ends meet financially anyway. It was down to Darwinism and simple numbers. The more we blocked, the more we got paid in bonuses. So she stood there for a moment and stared daggers at me, hands on hips.

'Go on then' I shrugged. 'Aint you going to spit on me?'

'What? Are you insane?' She smiled nervously. 'I'm not going to spit at you!'

'Then shut-up and join me for a drink tonight!' She looked at me dumbfounded.

'You are insane.' She laughed. 'No-friken-way!'

'Right' I sighed. 'ok...'

There was nothing for it now but to give her a final ultimatum. I indicated at the big red button on my desk and told her that if she didn't comply, I would press it.

'And what does that do exactly?'

'Oh it turns your tag off.'

'Seriously? You're going to block me? Is that it?'

'Choice is yours love. Either give us a kiss or I block your tag. And mind you, you don't wanna be stuck outdoors tonight love, not with the festival kicking off. Anything could happen!'

She regarded the big red button and gulped. I smiled. Actually it operated the coffee machine. But she didn't know that.

'I'd rather kiss a dead friken frog covered in excrement!' She said. (or words to that effect). I hovered my hand over the now glowing red button, poised to press it. Her eyes widened. Suddenly she changed her tune and surrendered to the logic of the situation.

'Alright! Jesus Christ! Ok! Ill friken do it' Finally. A result. Of course she was never going to kiss me, they never did. They always spat at you, (even the good looking ones like her). I would block her anyway, then turn her in for being a dissident and get my juicy bonus, which would sort me out for that evenings night of revelry. It was a win-win.

I looked forward to a night of wild debauchery. There was of course the sex-tents opening in Hyde park at seven o'clock. Although, I would need to get myself rather mullered to get to that state of mind (and seldom I remembered any of it in the past anyway).

I rose from my desk, removed the lower part of my face-mask and leant forward, puckering my lips. Still wearing those stupid red goggles, I closed my eyes and awaited.

My eyes still firmly closed, I put my hands on the desk and leant in closer, awaiting for her beautiful phlegm to flob across my semi-covered face.

Terry often had a sound-effect that went k-ching whenever he was gobbed at, like coins falling or something. I think it was an app but it was very funny. Anyway. I waited and waited but nothing happened.

Then, to my utter disbelief, I felt her lips pressed against mine and her warm and lascivious tongue forcing its way into my mouth. Exploring it's new found surroundings, her writhing organ rolled and writhed as her lips locked onto mine in sweet ecstasy.

Jeeze. In this moment, I lost all sense of all time, of where I was and what I was doing. The bonus and the office of Imitons melted away and for a moment, I found myself floating with her in a maelstrom of swirling ecstasy, with cartoon butterflies, accompanied by Beethoven's climax to *Ode to Joy*.

So much so that I almost didn't realise that she stabbed me through the back of my right hand, with my own friken pen.

*

Suddenly, the cartoon butterflies and Beethoven vanished, as a loud thud rumbled my ears. My eyes flickered wide open and began to smart with the pain.

A whole range of emotions ran through my being, from surprise, to fear, to utter dumbfoundedness and of course absolute agony. The pain was quite indescribable but the next thing I remember was screeching and roaring.

Mainly because the pen had not only rammed thru my hand but had punctured the big red friken button beneath. With a shower of sparks it suddenly activated the coffee machine. Quickly a panel drew back in the desk and the coffee machine slid up.

It proceeded to pour boiling hot water where a cup should have been placed on the big red button. But instead my hand was there, scolding me in scorching Espresso or Americano. I can't remember which. Screaming and cursing, I struggled to pull away until finally I freed myself from the table. But my hand was still skewered with blood and hot coffee, which ran up my arm and splattered upon the grey carpets. At this point, the woman in black backed away, covering her mouth.

'YOU!' I cried in disbelief. 'You - you stabbed me!'

'I'm ...I'm so sorry!' She said retreating towards the exit. 'I didn't mean to!'

I stared in horror at the bloody digi-pen now protruding through my hand. It had mangled my tag-implant for sure. I tried to pull the pen out but it hurt like hell. Best to leave it.

Perhaps she realised what she had done even before I did. It was the lowest of the low. The worst of the worst. Getting my tag replaced would take forever. But presently quelling the pain was my chief concern.

The last I saw of her, was pushing the Imitons aside, as she fled the office for dust.

The exit door swung back and forth in her wake. And she was gone.

Oh Terry. How had it come to this? I slumped in my chair, bleeding all over my desk in agony. And there it was on the work top: my tag implant, smeared in blood. Little more now than twisted tin-foil. Suddenly my life flashed before me.

Without my tag, there was no way I could get a train back home now. I was effectively stranded! I couldn't even get a bus, let alone a taxi! How the hell was I supposed to get back tonight without it? And the festival! Oh god. It would be starting soon! And my regular clothes! Oh jesus. Now trapped in the locker! With no way for me to access them! I couldn't very well blunder across London on foot, still dressed in my work overalls? I'd be killed for sure! And even if I did make it home. How was I supposed to get inside? Not to mention buying food? Or paying my bills? I was utterly and royally screwed.

Meanwhile all the Imitons were facing me, not lifting a finger to help. I demanded medical attention. But they just stood there, silent, like so many shop-window dummies.

It was almost as if they couldn't see me. Like I had suddenly ceased to exist. In any event, this would be the start of a very, very long night. But that would soon prove to be the least of my worries...

About the author

JS Adams has been writing science Fiction and fantasy for quite some time now. Each of his stories is autobiographic in some way or another. He enjoys dressing the "now" in the *what if?*
Inspired by the likes of HG Wells, John Wyndham, George Orwell, and Carl Sagen, he is a fervent vocal advocate for positive political change, for a fairer and better world. As a result, many of his stories raise issues regarding economic crises and the needs for social reforms. Jsadams-writer@outlook.com
Published on Kindle.

'Inscription' by Fiona Ballard

Introduction

Beatrice Gardiner's family gather round her bedside. "The ring," she whispers, with a collapsing exit breath. Fabienne takes the simple gold band from her mother's scrawny finger; she finds the inscription with two dates, three months apart. The backdrop for this tale of intrigue and divided family loyalties. Would Ralph step up or cower in the shadows, losing credibility with his offspring? Samuel Gardiner, removed from Beatrice at birth and sent for adoption, begins digging into his past. When solicitors notify him that his mother has passed, he swoops in on the grieving family causing mayhem. Baffled resentment soon turns to rage when he discovers he has three siblings who stand to inherit the major share of their mother's estate. What could be sweeter than to pit his step-brother and sisters against each other and carve out his own inheritance? Samuel circles the family, searching for points of weakness.

Extract

Chapter 1 Beatrice – 1999

The nearest oncology department, at the Dorset Infirmary, lay over thirty miles away from Ocean Cottage. The appointment letter had arrived two weeks before. She'd hidden it, deciding not to worry Ralph. It would probably be nothing to fret about anyway. Fabienne, her eldest, had offered to drive her. Caught up in their own thoughts, Beatrice chose to concentrate on the beauty of the surrounding countryside in order to take her mind off the impending appointment. Fabienne had been considering her next house move. They remained silent for the entire journey, which was unusual. The drive took them past Corfe Castle, where the family had spent many happy hours. After negotiating the unhelpful one-way system through the market town they parked up outside the sign for the mortuary. Fabienne got them there early, with fifteen minutes to spare.

As Beatrice glanced up at the hospital signage she asked herself why placing the mortuary alongside an oncology department was good estate planning. As they walked the long empty corridor down to the oncology department, the mother and daughter role shifted from one to the other as Fabienne took her hand. For a brief moment she regretted not telling Ralph where she was going. She'd told him only half a lie when he'd asked. The waiting area smelt of plastic and recent disinfectant as she helped herself to a small cup of water in a cone-shaped cup. At ten o'clock, a receptionist called out her name.

"Ms Gardiner? This way please." Smiling, making incessant small talk. The two women stood up and followed behind. The nurse, in the crisp burgundy uniform with white piping, stood alongside Mr Markham, who held out his hand, offering a firm handshake. Laid out in a fan shape on his desk: the recent kidney scan results.

"I'm guessing it's not good news?" Her voice is soft.

"Well, it's not as bad as we'd originally thought. Your scan shows that you do have an eight-millimetre tumour on your right kidney. It is treatable with a minor op and with the correct drugs we can remove it. If it turns out to be benign, that'll be all the treatment you will need. If it turns out to be cancerous you'll need to return for further treatment. But let's wait for the biopsy results, shall we, and not jump too far ahead? They should tell us a bit more." She warmed to his calming manner, found it reassuring. A short-sleeved shirt showed off a recent tan on his forearms. He must like the outdoor life, she thought, trying to distract any naughtier thoughts seeping into her mind. The word "cancer" had never featured in her vocabulary, not a word that many people spoke about. Beatrice knew nobody else who had it. He went on to say, "I'm aware it must be a shock to discover you have a tumour, but kidney ones are quite common."

"How long will I have to wait for the operation?" she asked, clutching her handbag. "The waiting time should be roughly four weeks and we should be able to fit you into the schedule, unless of course you want to take a cancellation?" She nodded "yes" to a cancellation; they all agreed it sounded a good idea. Words failed to describe the joyous feeling as she emerged that everything was going to be ok, and she would make a full recovery. Why trouble Ralph with all this stuff? He'd never been good at emotional stuff. The news came as a relief, because as usual Beatrice had feared the worst.

She didn't want to think negative thoughts and had already made up her mind that the tumour would be benign. She managed to hold back a few tears of relief as they made their way out to the car park. Fabienne offered to collect the car and pick up her mother from the bench outside oncology. Beatrice sat waiting patiently for Fabienne on the hospital bench as instructed.

It seemed the perfect moment to pounce. Samuel had been watching the scenario play out, and chosen his moment exactly to coincide with Beatrice being alone. He heard her voice for the first time and instantly warmed to the soft intonation. He sat down alongside and commented unprompted on the warmth of the sunshine.

"I love the sun at this time of year."

"Sorry, do I know you?" Beatrice hesitated, glancing sideways.

"No, we've not met. My name is Samuel."

Beatrice's face swung across, shocked, before turning ashen, instantly feeling faint. Her vision tunnelled into fine black pinpricks. The cars ahead started to spin, as she clung to the arm of the bench. For a brief moment she closed her eyes. This was surely one of her bad dreams. Could this person be the baby she was forced to give up at birth? How had he traced her to this bench?

"Sorry, I didn't mean to frighten you," continued the bearded man, running his hands through his thick, dark hair.

"I'll be ok, just give me a second. My daughter will be back in a moment. She's gone to get the car."

"Your daughter, ah?" He stroked his bearded chin. She had a fleeting moment to ask the loaded question.

"So, where are you living these days? Are you local?" He didn't answer straight away.

"Nowhere; actually I don't have a home." Lying came easily. Beatrice immediately took pity on him, as her heart started to melt.

"You must have a home." After a long silence, Samuel deliberated whether to tell more lies or simply wind up the conversation and flee. He didn't fancy meeting any step siblings at that point. Jesus, his plan had all gone horribly wrong.

"This was such a bad idea. Perhaps I could ring you to arrange a better location for another time?" He stood up to leave, buttoning up his coat.

"Yes, yes that's much better." As his voice trailed off, he watched her scribble her home number on an envelope. Samuel hadn't meant to snatch it, but walked quickly away without looking back, towards the bus stop and the perimeter fence. Tucked inside the envelope was the appointment letter with her home address at the top on the right. That was all he needed. Bingo.

From a distance Beatrice thought he looked like a vagrant. Like the ones that seek shelter in shop doorways at night. His old navy greatcoat looked torn, the collar fraying at the edges. The shoes looked worse, worn down on the soles. His gait had been akin to Jack's. But nothing a good bath and a hair wash wouldn't sort out, ran through her mind. Fabienne pulled into the lay-by and wound down the car window.

"You ok, Mum? You look awfully pale. Who was that man?" Beatrice didn't answer and got in the car. Her brain immediately went into meltdown.

How the hell did Samuel know she would be at the hospital at that time? She hoped he hadn't been stalking her. Was Ralph in on the secret even though she hadn't told him where she was going? Random threads cut across her mind, without any foundation or endings. After a slow drive home, Fabienne suggested she cook them lunch as Ralph was out with their neighbour, Freddie. Food always interested Beatrice in whatever form. Pork chops and a couple of wrinkled apples for a sauce would suffice. They stopped off at the village shop to buy some cream.

With stomachs replete, mother and daughter headed down to the beach. Beatrice swam in the sea, and Fabienne lay on a towel reading her book. By late afternoon her mood had brightened and conversations turned to a lighter tone. When Ralph returned, they retired to bed, sticking to their familiar bedtime routine. Whilst she undressed and brushed her teeth she wondered whether she should share the hospital incident with him yet or keep it to herself. Perhaps he knew about it already. She decided to review her decision in the morning when her mind would be thinking more clearly and less befuddled by wine and strong emotions.

※

Three months later the family had gathered around her hospital bed. Had she had a premonition about her own mortality? Perhaps it had been the real reason for the sudden change of heart? Curled up in a foetal position, she uttered three faint words: "Fabienne, the ring." The family looked up at one another, bemused. Her thick lashes fluttered. Her mouth fell open as though she wanted to say something; but her mind thought better of it. On the other side of the bed stood Ralph Barclay, holding her cool, limp hand, gently smoothing the flattened blue veins under his thumb.

"Rest now," he told her. Together the assembled group thought they had worked out the meaning of her mumblings. The room, although chilly, felt calm; soft music played in the background on the sound system. The morphine started enhancing her hallucinations again, as she fell deeply into the weirdest of dreams. Her brain questioned if this was real?

With her feet secured firmly in the stirrups she held the reins high, using her calves to urge the horse forward. It responded into a brisk canter. The pale sandy beach spread across the bay for three miles. The vast expanse fired up the chestnut filly to whinny with excitement, kicking out her hind legs. The rider clung tightly to the martingale as the horse sped up. Released from captivity and ready to charge. As they turned into the wind her black mane rippled as their speed increased. The rider going too fast, chasing someone or being chased herself? In the distance stood a solitary figure... in a black cassock and matching Romano cap. Wasn't that Father O'Flynn holding a baby wrapped in a yellow shawl? Shouting into the wind, her voice mute. She pulled up and dismounted, ready to take her baby, but when her feet touched the ground the dark figure holding the baby had vanished. Scanning the horizon, her hand to her forehead, the darkened form resembling the priest had faded.

She awoke to find her bed sheets and nightdress drenched in perspiration. Someone with cool hands had changed her into a dry nightie. How long had she been asleep? The inside of her mouth felt as dry as an old sponge. With her heart still racing, she pressed the button that powered the syringe driver pump, topping up her morphine. The horse ride dream had taken its toll on her strength and she fell back on the pillows, deep into the black hole of more hallucinations. She had always had a deep-rooted fear that she would end up dying alone. Where was he? Who asked a voice? This time she felt a different hand, familiar, larger, more callused. The morphine muddling her crazy thoughts and somewhere in her confusion she'd lost Ralph.

Beatrice had chosen this particular hospice room for its light, to facilitate a peaceful end. An archetypal hospice room with bland decor, tired magnolia walls, an eighties throwback. The windows had metal frames and leaded glass windows. The garden doors swung open onto a terrace. In one of her more lucid moments she relished the cool breeze that drifted through and requested the nurses leave it ajar.

Ralph rechecked his watch: three minutes past three. His beloved Beatrice had just taken her last breath; he allowed himself a muffled sob into his hankie, piercing the silence. The two daughters hugged their father, standing side by side like small children holding hands. Their brother, Douglas, stood on the fringes of the family group, attempting to keep his emotions in check, furiously chewing the inside of his cheek. The door opened as the portly nurse came bustling in, followed by a doctor who asked them to wait outside.

Douglas fled and sought sanctuary in a small corner of the hospice garden. Lighting up, even though the forbidden signs were directly in his eyeline. They were no deterrent. At the rear of the main building he found a low brick wall opposite a large stone feature. So, paused a moment, taking the first drag, he cast his eye over the dozen or more large grey stone boulders in front of him. Trying to puzzle out what they were meant to be. Flattish in shape, laid out in such a pattern to form a walled structure. A steady trickle of water cascaded from the middle stone, streaming neatly into a small fountain. The water feature cleverly drew the eye to the centrepiece as the clear liquid spilled out towards the rectangular pool below. Douglas had read about landscape gardening in a magazine. This particular garden seemed different, though. Vibrant colours splashed around the edges from the carefully positioned plants and shrubs alongside ferns and fuchsias. Obviously it had been built with a calming influence in mind, by an experienced landscape gardener.

    He drew so hard on his cigarette it sizzled; exhaling the smoke into rings, as he attempted to gather his thoughts. The first of which, "well, how unexpected." He wished he'd taken the hint from his father and visited his mother sooner. Over the last few months he had become more estranged from his family. He held back his tears, scowling in a manly sort of way. Unsure, as emotions didn't fit his toughened persona. Recently he had left his elder sister's calls unanswered, isolating himself further. Today was not the time for recriminations. His phone number had changed so regularly that it made communication difficult. A feeble excuse. Regrets tumbled loosely among his thoughts, too many to consider in one go. Who would he have shared those personal thoughts with anyway? Certainly not Molly, the latest girlfriend.

He'd also felt hurt when Fabienne had referred to him as flaky. What had she meant by that? He knew he'd been given everything as a youngster, but pushed it all away. The memory of Beatrice defending him in an argument with his sister, came to mind. Always looking for danger, and risk mixed with a little heroism. Not too much to ask? He'd failed to notice his second cigarette had come to an abrupt end. Either he lit up another or returned inside to deal with reality. Shivering, he thought it easier to stay outside, where nobody could push him into playing a dutiful part. He had nobody directing him in thoughts or actions. Knowing that Molly was back at the cottage on her own, that would do as an excuse, to escape the oppressive, sterile atmosphere inside.

"Ah, there you are, Douglas. We've decided to make our way home," Ralph announced. Douglas heard it as "The royal *we*; I'm still your dad and can tell you what to do, *we*". Ralph couldn't tell if his son was upset or not.

"Sorry, are you ready to leave, or do you want to go back in the room alone for a few moments?" Ralph, feeling charitable, looked at him expectantly.

"No thanks, I'm done with this hellish place." He was content to remember his mother as she had been in the days before, relaxed and happy, surrounded by her family. Why hang around? There seemed little point, as the focus of their attention had departed. The small party of four silently made their way back to Molly, waiting at the cottage. The atmosphere at home felt strange, as Beatrice was ostensibly still there. Everything as she had left it a few hours before. Coats hanging in the hallway, boots by the back door, a coffee cup with lip balm around the rim on the table. No clearing up had been done, despite Fabienne's firm instructions to Molly, who had been luxuriating in a lavender bubble bath and reading magazines.

Molly opened the door, the dragon tattoo clearly visible on her chest, loosely covered by a cheesecloth shirt. She rushed to hug Douglas close to her in the hallway. He'd badly needed some fresh sea air and another fag. So he took her hand and pulled her out into the garden, where he explained that he wanted to hit the road earlier than they'd planned.

A man of few words, Ralph watched them through the kitchen window and felt struck by

Douglas's tenderness towards the girl that none of them really knew. He had never witnessed his son with a proper grown-up girlfriend and thought they seemed in tune with one another. Over the weekend he'd felt a renewed closeness between Douglas and himself but may have misread the signals.

※

Eloise, the youngest sibling, was born with baby blue eyes that sparkled when she laughed. She kept her hair short and its original blonde colour still held firm. Her beatific smile caught people by surprise. People remarked that her facial expressions were also akin to her father's and sometimes her laugh too, the manner of it rather than the tone. Blessed with a gentle sprinkling of pale freckles across the bridge of her nose that highlighted themselves during the summer. Her trim waistline had thickened slightly after years spent cooking and sampling food in the French kitchens. The long working hours meant she didn't get outside to exercise as much as she would like. Her daily routine was now firmly governed by the restaurant bookings for dinners, rather than a regular exercise routine.

Her childhood memories consisted of playing on the beach at Ocean Cottage, running around the garden and playing in the tree house with her friends. Followed by eating tea on paper plates up in the tree house, with strawberry jam sandwiches, chocolate mini-rolls, and apples sliced straight from the orchard. The children made posters deterring the adults from entry and wrote: NO ENTRY OR DEFF with a wonky skull and crossbones at the bottom. They used yards and yards of Sellotape to attach it to the ladder at the bottom.

The darker memories came when she thought of her brother. Being shoved over on the gravel by Douglas, who quickly became jealous of his new baby sister staggering around outside learning to squat down and balance. The pain to her kneecaps as she went down, and the scream for help. Douglas caused her to tumble over when he thought his mother might be looking the other way. His baby sister ended up covered in bruises and bashes. He liked to snatch her toys away, causing her to sob until Fabienne or Beatrice would notice and chastise him offering her back her pet toy. Douglas enjoyed snatching her toys away causing her to sob until Beatrice would take pity on her and offer her treasured toy back. When Beatrice raised it as a concern with the health visitor she classed it as normal sibling rivalry behaviour.

As soon as Douglas could verbalise his feelings he told his baby sister firmly. "Go home, baby, no like you," as he opened the front door, the toddling baby now exposed to freedom. By chance Beatrice came through the hallway to the living room and noticed the open door. Stepping outside, she found Eloise in the flowerbed picking the heads off the daffodils. Despite the locked gates to the beach it had made Beatrice's heart miss a beat. How did the toddler open the front door? The clue: the small chair that Douglas used to allow his sister some fresh air.

※

Of the three siblings Eloise proved to be the most sentimental. Often reserving her opinion for fear of being shouted down or drowned out by the more forceful personalities around her. As a teenager she became withdrawn, moody in the usual sort of way. She left home without going to university and took herself off to France to work and study. Perhaps it had been a subconscious decision to live abroad and distance herself from family dramas and conflict. Even-tempered and not known to overdramatise events or situations, unlike her sister.

Romuel, the love of her life, would take her away from her kitchen duties and encourage out onto the water in France. Her father had taught her to sail, so she had grown up without a fear of the open sea. They would take trips out to the undiscovered islands off the west coast. She loved nothing more than to dive off the boat and sink as deep as her lungs would allow, resurfacing in the shape of a mermaid. The water brought the pair calm, after the stresses of working at the restaurant.

They'd met as teenagers whilst working in the kitchens of a large family run hotel, Eloise working as a sous-chef and Romuel as a waiter serving evening covers. They formed an instant connection and found they had much in common. He had been her first real love since arriving in France. Her ambition: to settle and take French citizenship, then train to be a chef at La Cuisine, Corsaire Ecole. He helped her achieve that dream. They went on to marry, and had their first child, Amélie. A bouncing, blonde, blue-eyed baby who cooed and gurgled at everyone she met. Born prematurely, the tot weighed only two kilos and spent the first month of her life in an incubator. Owing to her early arrival the baby's weight was slight. Her petit nose came later with a tiny piercing on the right-hand side of her nostril, near her freckles. Her eyes akin to her grandfather's, with extended dark lashes that curled naturally she had inherited a happy-go-lucky personality. Amélie became their pride and joy.

A year later Eloise miscarried a second baby at thirteen weeks after falling down a step outside the restaurant, landing awkwardly on her side. The doctors advised her not to have any more babies.

La Baule had become a chic upmarket seaside resort in the Seventies. A quaint mix of old and Breton seaside cultures. The restaurants dotted along the twelve-kilometre beach, alongside a swish yachting marina, were testament to the wealth and status of its locals. The French family lifestyle meant they spent their winters skiing. Apart from inheriting her mother's phobia for insects and spiders, Amelie sailed through her teenage years with ambitious plans to go travelling. Recently she had hooked up with Guy, who had passed the parental acid test with flying colours. But those plans were interrupted by an unplanned pregnancy followed by another in quick succession.

If Eloise had one regret about settling in France, it was that she didn't get over to England, to spend time with her parents. Time off from the kitchen proved difficult to secure, and the added complication of distance. Looking back she felt her emotional burdens had always been linked to past family conflicts. For Eloise during those years back home, she'd tried her hardest to avoid any serious conflict or melee. Choosing to tuck herself away in her bedroom, reading or listening to her radio, or strumming her guitar as music became her solace.

Obituary – September 1999

The obituary filled the back page of the *Swanage Echo*. The newspaper column showed an old black-and-white grainy picture of Beatrice in her youth. Ralph had picked his favourite photo of her leaning against a wall holding a bicycle and throwing her head back with laughter. Her hair tied up in a gingham headscarf, wearing blue denim dungarees, it seemed to sum her up beautifully as it captured her perfect smile.

It is with great sadness that Ralph Barclay and family of Ocean Cottage, Swanage, wish to announce the death of Beatrice Hamilton, beloved partner and mother to their three children. Born in Consett, County Durham, in 1949, Beatrice was one of four siblings, Arthur, Albert, and Rosina. She had led a colourful life at home and abroad in France, and always put others before herself. The burial service will take place at St Cuthbert's Church on Friday, September 18th, at 12 noon. The family asks for no flowers. All donations to Barnardo's Children's Homes.

About the author

To date Fiona has written a semi-autobiography, Taking The Bandage. A book of short stories, The Wedding Dress. An adult Mystery/Drama novel, Look Both Ways. Inscription, was released in January 2024. The latest book, Malachi & the Sick Dragon will be released on March 1st. Fiona currently belongs to the The Writers Hub & Portsmouth Authors Collective, an eclectic mix of local authors. It offers training and support in addition to promotional book sales events. All books can be purchased via ballardsbookshelf.com

'Unjudging Love: The Enigma of Dylan Thomas' by Josh Brown

Introduction

The Enigma of Dylan Thomas is a groundbreaking re-examination of the life and work of the great Welsh poet published by Away With Words Press in 2024. It was launched in Swansea in the house where Thomas was born, 5 Cymdonkin Drive by a televised interview with the author Alun Gibbard. The book examines the complex realities of the life and personality of the poet behind the popular misconceptions of a drunken womaniser who hates his native land and argues that his work was based on deeply held metaphysical convictions and centuries old traditions of Welsh bardic poetry. It is a refreshingly new vision of the poet and his wife Caitlin profoundly critical of previous biographies and contains several previously unknown or ignored facts about them both. Written over four years of research, the book takes its title from the closing lines of the poem 'This side of the truth' written to his six year old son Llewelyn - "Water and light, the earth and sky, / Is cast before you move. / And all your deeds and words, / Each truth, each lie, / Die in unjudging love." The book retails at £15 and is available from independent booksellers and online.

Extract

From Chapter 4 Sailing Toward Death

Of the hundreds of letters Dylan Thomas wrote, one to Margaret Taylor about the prospect of moving back to Laugharne is the most joyous and poetic, full of childish glee at the prospect of living in Castle House in Laugharne. Of all possible words only 'glee' suits the childlike excitement. All his faults and charm derived from the fact that, at heart, he never really grew up. This letter was testament to that. For all his desire to be the wunderkind bohemian poet which took him repeatedly to the sleazy avant garde quarters of London, he was only comfortable in the safety of Wales and the child land towns of Aber Taf, home of aunts, cousins, and ancestors, his perfect refuge. Dylan's rhapsody was premature, it would be several months before he and the family would return to the one place he had always felt most himself and then not to the world's best street with its cherry trees as he expected but somewhere more unique and suited to the poet. Somewhere priested by herons, with hedgerows of joy. Earlier that autumn, Dylan had written to Frances Hughes to enquire if Castle House, which she and her author husband Richard had left, was available to rent. This was an opportunity for the doting Margaret to serve once again to rescue him and keep him tied in gratitude to her. She travelled to Laugharne to negotiate on his behalf prompting this wonderful letter. Castle House was not available but undismayed she continued her quest to find suitable, inspiring accommodation for her protégé. She found it. The Boathouse.

Laugharne was and still is a curious village of a town, thirteen miles from Carmarthen via the nearby town of St Clears on small rural roads through gentle green countryside. Surrounded by Welsh-speaking villages, it was almost entirely English speaking with a distinctly non-Welsh history. Its unusual character arose probably from its isolation not only as a small country town or its inaccessibility (it had no railway station), but also as an unfathomable English enclave in West Wales, the principality of Deheubarth which had been split into three counties by Edward the first in the Statute of Rhuddlan. Hardly more than a huddle of houses, it is the only surviving medieval corporation other than the City of London, presided over by a Portreeve. And what magnificent houses some of them are, expansive beautiful houses on whose walls one drunken night you might graffito 'Library' to remind the closeted town of the location of its books. Laugharne had its foot so firmly in its past it was also one of only two places in the UK to still have land farmed under the 'open field system'. Was it any wonder it was both beguiling and barmy (both spellings of course)? Dylan would have felt comforted here. It was Wales but an Anglicised Wales. It was beautiful, if you were not one of the farm workers or cockle pickers who scraped a meagre subsistence from it. It had eccentricity and a rural poshness about it making it attractive to Welsh artists. Laugharne was somewhere begging to be gentrified. A magnificent town peopled by curiosities set in the Taf estuary with views across to Llansteffan on the Towy. It was Dylan's hiraeth that drew him back, not just to Wales but to this part of Wales and the Boathouse was the perfect location for him. Not just because of its spectacular position but because it mirrored the position in his world his genius needed. Safely, snugly, entrapped in a small space but looking out onto a large world was central to his view of life and a metaphor of his craft and poetry bringing into the world what was deep within. And it came with the perfect fixture. Dylan had always written in small, confined spaces with magnificent views. A bedroom next to the boiler in Uplands Swansea. Hughes' pagoda in the castle, the summer house in Blashford, a caravan in Oxford and now, a little garage built for a doctor's car on the rock face above the house. A writing shed complete with herons.

Visited today, you realise what attracted writers and artists to the town, it has the euphemistic picture postcard prettiness that enchants literary tourists. But they visit in the clement months or stay in modernised cottages. They do not see the isolated town on a damp winter evening, do not consider the inconveniences of living in a place where the nearest real approximation to a supermarket is a bus journey away. They see the Boathouse modernised into a museum not a damp rat-ridden house with no heating. It is an impressive house, with an upper garden down from the path and a lower garden and terrace backed into the cliff face on a walled shelf. Three storeys high, a wooden balcony runs around it above the ground floor with steps down to the lower garden. The gate to the sea path disappeared some years ago and was found in the mud by children, one of them a young Michael Sheen the Welsh actor. For all its stunning location, the Boathouse with its first-floor balcony and its base in the tidal mud was not an ideal or safe place in which to bring up small children. This at a time when his fame was spreading, and new challenges were about to arrive from across the Atlantic. Yet, despite this and the continual money worries, the first months in the new home were apparently happy. The garage was converted by Caitlin into the 'writing shed' with a coal-fired burner in the winter and a table and chair facing a window that looked out over the estuary which she had installed. Here Dylan worked in closeted contentment writing, refining, and re-writing his poems and the play for voices he had been carrying for several years. Aeronwy Thomas would recall listening to her father in the shed reciting lines out loud over and over to get them right. It would be the last period of true happiness in his marriage. The chameleon would take over their lives. The image become a self-destructive demon.

A fortnight after they settled in Laugharne a letter arrived from New York from a young poet and admirer. He had read of Dylan's desire to come to America and, having just been made Director of the Poetry Centre at the 92nd Street 'Y' (Young Men's and Young Women's Hebrew Association), was now able to make that possible. Dylan wrote back immediately accepting and asking John Malcolm Brinnin to arrange other readings in the USA. His American agent had no experience of such an undertaking so Brinnin (though he was equally inexperienced) took on the role at a 15% fee. A crippling programme was arranged covering the US and into Canada which an experienced tour director might have known was impossible to sustain. Anyone who knew Dylan's state of health certainly would. Possibly Dylan felt refreshed and invigorated by the months in sleepy Laugharne. At the beginning of 1950, he wrote to Princess Caetani to answer her fears about his drinking, joking that it frightened him too.

A month later, he had to send an urgent letter to Caitlin from London because he had left his passport and cheque book in the writing shed and only realised when he was on the train. They went to a farewell party where he became extremely drunk. On February 20th he flew to New York, arriving with a terrible hangover and the ill effects of the flight. The romantic promise of Laugharne was over, and the fatal, collapsing period of his life had begun. The myth was about to engulf him, and his chameleon self would push him toward a tawdry version of his self-fulfilling prophesy of poet doomed to die young.

You belong to NY instantly, unlike any other place on earth. You have seen a hundred movies, a thousand TV series set in NYC, heard dozens of songs, read novels and poems about mean streets and leafy squares. Deborah Kerr runs up W34th street to a fateful date with Cary Grant. Sinatra is leaving today to be on the town. Up from the Friends apartment block on the corner of Bedford, Bob Dylan walked hunched in a suede jacket through the Village and the poet he stole his name from drank famously with stevedores. Like a perfect infection, New York is dormant in the blood, a place you know well even if you've never been. But New York is still a surprise. The plane comes down over the marsh and flatlands of Rockaway with its beachfront cottages into the cluster of airports that is now JFK. The clapboard houses of Queens are Rockwell smalltown. Maybe the yellow cab is no longer driven by a guy from the Bronx, the freeway needs repair and, as it approaches, Manhattan is a smaller compact copy of the place you've seen in so many photographs. Yet viewed from the Queensboro Bridge it is amazing, breath taking, a wonderous visual parody of itself clawing the skyline with concrete, glass, and neon, full of mystery and promise and as F. Scott Fitzgerald said in The Great Gatsby, like the first time.

So, it must have been when Dylan Thomas rumbled in after crossing the Atlantic, 'pond'. Doubtless he must have remembered Ezra Pound's description of night in the city that never slept, the poetry of the night lit city as if the stars had been pulled down. You want to tell the cab driver to stop on the 'great white way' or take you an Irish bar for pastrami and bourbon. You want to sit down and weep in Grand Central. You want to head to Hudson and spend time in the White Horse! New York is a familiar surprise, a fabulous cliché. A city of villages, each proud and distinct. A city so diverse, so self-assured it is not America but a country of its own. Utterly Jewish, as Italian as Napoli and so Irish the whole five boroughs celebrate St Patrick in a massive green festival. Built by immigrants who fought to have their place, and it shows. The music is black jazz written by Jewish guys. The Kosher food is Lower East Side Italian. It's the ultimate melting pot where, amazingly, people remain both fiercely proud of their roots and of being New Yorkers. New York defies its stereotypes. The people are friendly, they smile on the sidewalk. The Empire State is plain, marked out by its height and presumptuous name. The skyscrapers that have not been torn down are achingly beautiful art deco merged with American Gothic. Forget Central Park, the smaller potters fields that are Bryant and Washington have more character, little green oases hemmed by glass and steel. Or Battery Park with its stunning monuments and view across the Hudson to Ms Liberty. Any boulevard of frighteningly tall buildings is a walk away from older streets of low tenements where you can still find locals clinging desperately to their communities in a city where spiralling prices threaten them into oblivion. You can stroll from Midtown to Greenwich Village between breakfast and lunch down 5th past the iconic Flatiron or meander from Grand Central, the Chrysler and Empire State. You can walk the Highline to it, redundant city steel turned into urban countryside. You can approach it from the Battery, Brooklyn Bridge or Wall Street. You might take Library Walk with its literary quotes set in metal on the sidewalk and find yourself stood on a stanza from 'In My Craft and Sullen Art' or another from Alfred Kazin brother of the woman Dylan was to fall fatally in love with.

Greenwich is a rich village now. The poets and hipsters, the folkniks, Beats and Kerouac wannabes are gone. Only the sign of the Village Gate remains. But the laid-back bohemian character has moved into the 21st century not disappeared. There are still longshoremen in James Dean's favourite bar. The cramped apartment over a sex shop on W4th where the other Dylan invented his myth with a battered suede jacket and a stolen name is still there. Tourists, university students and locals take selfies in the sunlight in Washington Park over the unnamed remains of more than twenty thousand dead, "huddled masses yearning to breathe free" who learned the cruel reality of the great dream that brought them to New York. Henry James lived here, and youth culture kicked off a whole decade before Presley learned to sing black music. It may have been cold the day Robert Zimmerman posed with Suze Rotolo for the cover of his second album but the way he hunched inside his leather jacket on Jones Street was stolen from James Dean photographed a decade earlier in Times Square for the Daily News. Washington Park grew over the creek that gave its name to the

Minetta Tavern, on the MacDougal Street of Kerouac's poem with its Gaslight and Wha Café's next door to the Minetta. The bearded young men are long gone but the venues cling to the memory of past glories of poets and rock legends. On the corner of MacDougal and Bleeker the San Remo Café was a less known haunt of Dylan Thomas along with pretty much every name in American literature of the 50's – Tennessee Williams, Alan Ginsberg, Gregory Corso, Jack Kerouac, James Baldwin and Gore Vidal. But the San Remo, the first place Dylan took a drink in New York City, no longer exists.

MacDougal crosses Bleeker Street immortalised by Paul Simon. Off Bleeker, the Cherry Lane Theatre is still a major NY venue with a long history of great playwrights from Thorton Wilder to Edward Albee. Beckett's Waiting for Godot premiered there, and Dylan read his work in 1952 though the show was nearly cancelled because he mislaid his poems. Just before Bleeker joins 8th Avenue is the White Horse Tavern on Hudson Street, New York's oldest wooden building and the one place in the city most associated with Dylan Thomas, more so than the Chelsea. Unlike the Minetta, it has stayed much the same, a Village pub that just happened to have known some famous customers. Just as the Grisly Pear refuses to exploit its Jimmy Dean connection, so the Horse ignores the many famous customers of its 50's and 60's heyday that included e.e. cummings, Norman Mailer, Jack Kerouac, Brendan Behan, and James Baldwin. The other Dylan, Leonard Cohen and the poet/singer Jim Morrison were drawn to the place by its Thomas association. Famously the Clancy Brothers (who played regularly at the Cherry Lane Theatre before becoming famous) after a sell-out Maddison Square concert, did a repeat performance in the tavern for its customers, for free!

Paradoxically, in 1968 the Welsh songstress Mary Hopkin had a hit with "Those Were the Days" a re-working of a Russian song by New York folksinger Gene Raskin a professor of architecture who performed in the White Horse with his wife. Themed, like Fern Hill, around nostalgic regret for a lost youth and its innocence the song opening recalls a tavern. That tavern was the Horse. Only Dylan Thomas is referenced in the inn. A poster for Under Milk Wood, some photos, and a painted copy of Bunny Adler's famous photograph of Dylan at the bar. If you avoid the peak hours on a weekday afternoon the tavern is likely populated by locals for whom its literary past is not the reason to be sat at that bar and for whom the Minetta today is a hateful travesty. Another White Horse irony are the notices in the window and over the bar warning that drunkenness will not be tolerated. No eighteen whiskey sessions! The last photo before he died was taken in the Horse of Dylan raising a tumbler of whiskey staring past the German landlord who holds another on the bar. Dylan is bloated, distracted, fag inevitably hanging from his other hand; he looks to be in his fifties not thirty-nine. Sadly, though smartly dressed in a dapper bowtie, there is little trace of the handsome youth in the thick cardigan from his Nora Summers photoshoot other than the tousled mop of curly hair.

On a cold New York afternoon, you can shut out the noise of the city that never sleeps. Find a snug corner to yourself. Ask the barman for two fingers of Bourbon (Old Granddad if it still existed) and raise a glass to Mr Thomas. Dylan went hoping to make some easy money not counting on a gruelling schedule or what was expected of him. To earn it he had, FitzGibbon explained, to play the role of Dylan Thomas that America already expected of him, the cliched part of the miscreant drunken genius their Hollywood framed idea of a bohemian rebel led them to anticipate. All those pub performances were now going to be repeated on a big screen scale. His chameleon personality was about to take charge of his life submerging the real Dylan Thomas. In America he was not a poet but an actor playing the movie screen drama of a poet. He meandered around bars and bookshops, talked to other poets, encouraged women to take him to bed and behaved outrageously, on cue, at literary parties. W.H. Auden chided Brinnin with a look for opening this Pandora's box. It would quickly take its toll of him. Surely he must have realised the superficiality of the poet image in the big screen world. There would be no respite. In London, he could always escape back to Wales and close and caring friends he could turn to. In America there was none of that, just an endless repetition of the no-good-boyo character, the 'poet-clown' he had saddled himself with, being lapped up by baying crowds lustful for the taint of genius impropriety. The result was what his first biographer Constantine FitzGibbon described as a destructive exhibitionism encouraged by a voyeuristic pleasure in the spectacle of a drunken celebrity.

Off Washington on the corner of MacDougal, Dylan and Caitlin stayed at the

Hotel Earle before transferring to the Hotel Chelsea after the Beekman threw him out for noisy partying! Dylan is on the long list of 20th century greats who made the Chelsea their home, a list that includes Warhol, Sid Vicious, Patti Smith and Leonard Cohen. Here Dylan met to plan the first recording that launched the audio book industry. A New York, as enchanting as a siren luring him to his death. From here he sailed out to die.

Today, we know only too miserably well, the distasteful lengths a prurient media will go in search of a 'story', the cruel malicious depths it will sink to. We have seen how it treated Princess Diana, the victims of Hillsborough, the innocent memory of Millie Dowler. We know how vile the 'free press' can be. In the early 1950's the public was less sophisticated in its understanding of what can masquerade as fact. Dylan Thomas would not have realised how rapacious the attention was, like a murderous animal smiling as its bore down on its prey. Recalling this on the tenth anniversary of his death, Wynford Vaughan Thomas described the US reporters as vultures whose tricks included bribing waiters to fill a room with of glasses of beer then telling Dylan there was a phone call in the room so they could get the picture that confirmed the myth. Dylan naïvely posed for the pho.tographs not wishing to offend and, possibly, too willing to play the role. The press were not the only vultures. Dylan was in the constant company of celebrities, culture-vultures, sycophants, wealthy 'arts patrons' and all the other assembled parasites he had first encountered at the International Surrealism Exhibition in 1936. These were not the eccentrics of Fitzrovia, not adoring, if needy, patrons like Margaret Taylor. The only respite from the daily vampiric onslaught was the company of other writers or to find somewhere peopled by ordinary folk who did not care if he was an infamous poet. That place became the White Horse Tavern a dockside bar shared by stevedores and poets. Here he could meet people like himself, people more interested in the poetry and the poet than the media fantasy.

During his four visits, Dylan met some of the greatest American poets of the day in the hip alternative quarter of New York, the NYC equivalent of Fitzrovia. Here he knew his ground, he could be his loveable, talented, flawed self among people who would judge his work not his performances. Two were notably significant for Dylan listed them as his favourite American poets of the time.

Theodore Roethke was someone Dylan had admired and wanted to meet before the America charade had even been proposed. They met on his first visit. They hit it off wonderfully. Roethke was another groundbreaking poet who loved life and drink and had his own demons to grapple with. His poetry has a similar intensity and passion, the same fixation with death. When Dylan died, he wrote in Encounter one of the best summations of the poet behind and despite the cliché. He had, he said, expected a prodigious Welsh drinker but what he met was a man who drank modestly whilst talking about poetry and Wales, life in America and crime writers like Dashiel Hammett, wandered bookshops or indulged his love of old Marx Brothers movies. Dylan destroyed himself in pursuit of his art but, Roethke said, needed no one to defend him.

The other he met and befriended in 1950 was e.e.cummings. Dylan requested to meet Cummings, another American whose work he admired, not realising the admiration was mutual and that he had been in the audience for Dylan's reading at the 92Y on February 23rd. Cummings was so overwhelmed by the performance he walked the streets for hours afterwards trying to absorb what he had witnessed. Those who know Dylan's recordings will understand that. After Dylan's death, Cummings was part of the committee to raise funds for Caitlin and the children. It was inevitable the two should be drawn to each other. Both were operating outside the accepted norms of poetry at the time. Both wrote about time and childhood. Both had the same metaphysical focus in their work.

While away, Dylan wrote regularly to Caitlin and his parents, letters suggesting that behind his bad-boy performances, America overwhelmed and frightened him. His letters to Caitlin were full of pleading love, far removed from the bad behaviour with women at the glitterati parties. The letters indicate that he knew that many of the baying crowd were hangers-on and that he had realised he faced a programme impractical and destructive. This took him to Washington, Chicago, San Francisco, and Vancouver before returning to the Hotel Earle on Washington Square, New York. He hated the flight out so opted to sail home on the new Queen Elizabeth. His letters to Caitlin, of course, would have to placate and reassure her; she would suspect he was misbehaving with other women and had long since shown her contempt for his playing roles to suit his audience. He returned without the income the trip was meant to finance. It would have been less had Brinnin not hidden 800 dollars in a handbag Dylan had bought for Caitlin. Dylan's generosity at the bar had wasted too much of it and he never mastered the currency. He earned thousands but little of it came home with him. Despite the impassioned letters, Caitlin's mistrust would prove to be justified. John Malcolm Brinnin, in the book he wrote after Dylan's death, 'Dylan Thomas in America', mentioned a brief liaison with a woman he called 'Doris' and a serious affair with another called 'Sarah' . His use of pseudonyms may have been tactful or as Caitlin suspected his being careful to avoid legal action. It was not until 2000 that her identity was revealed in a Dylan Thomas biography. She was the first real love after Caitlin and her name was Pearl Kazin.

About the author

Josh Brown is a poet, author and podcaster born outside Wrexham in North Wales. The son of a coal miners' daughter and a chef, Josh grew up with poetry and music fused with a love of food and the only books he owns permanently are cookery and poetry.

Though his grandparents made the decision not to bring up his Mam and her sisters as Welsh speakers she retained her glorious song-bidden accent undimmed until her dying 94th year bequeathing him the hiraeth of Wales with its heart aching beauty, music, pride, rebellion, and poetry. With no close English translation, hiraeth is a longing which connects the Welsh with their homeland. Brought up in kitchens with daily talk of food he learned to cook and that the table is the nucleus of family and love. His first poems were published at seventeen and he was part of the early stand-up poetry scene but after college, worked in a factory, for an airline, and taught in a primary school before going to university to study economics.

Josh lectured in Business and Management in colleges and universities specialising in marketing, market research, statistical analysis, and business in the EU. In 2003 he was made a Fellow of the Royal Society of Arts. In the 1980's he co-formed a youth theatre company and performed on the Edinburgh Festival Fringe. Shortly before retiring he was Chair of the New Theatre Royal Portsmouth overseeing its renovation in partnership with the University of Portsmouth. In 2016 he and a friend Liz Weston founded Portsmouth

Poetry building a reputation for innovative community and educational projects, and supporting new, rising, and established poets in the UK and abroad. In 2023, they published their first collection of fifteen poets, 'Ecstasy & Grief'. Josh lives with his wife Marion in Southsea. Unjudging Love is dedicated to her and their dog Ruby and has a foreword by Patti Smith. On completion of the book, he had 'Hiraeth' tattooed on his forearm.

'Getting the Measure of Things' by Patsy Collins

Introduction

This complete short story is set in the picturesque seaside village of Little Mallow in Hampshire – the location of Patsy's cosy mystery series. It features some of the characters you'll find in those books. The titles, in order, are Disguised Murder and Community Spirit in Little Mallow, Dependable Friends and Deceitful Neighbours in Little Mallow and Deadly Words and Innocent Gossip in Little Mallow.

A short story 'Getting the Measure of Things'

Reverend Jerry Grande, vicar of St Symeon's church, walked around the village of Little Mallow. It was a glorious afternoon. The gardens filled with towering sunflowers looked magnificent, and everyone was in good spirits. It was the kind of day which made Jerry want to sing a hymn of praise. As he was within earshot of others he refrained.

Several of those parishioners he met were, like him, craning their necks to admire the cheerful sunflowers. A lot of people were outside chatting to friends or neighbours.

"Such lovely colours," Ellie Jenkins said when Jerry reached the garden she was gazing into.

"They are, yes," Jerry agreed. "But no more so than your own display. I particularly like the very rich orange one near your front gate – it's the exact shade of my favourite waistcoat."

"Oh yes!" Her pretty eyes sparkled and her lips twitched. "I think the flower is a little less bright, but I knew it reminded me of something." She made a slight attempt to suppress a giggle.

"Will you share the joke?" Jerry asked.

"Well, it's just... I got my seeds a bit mixed up and thought that was going to be a short white one. That's why I planted it amongst the mauve Busy Lizzies and pink petunias. Mary Milligan remarked that it wasn't quite in tune with the other blooms."

Jerry chuckled. "Not in tune! Yes, I see. I'd have thought that would bring me to mind straight away!"

"Oh, it did! I was just puzzled about why the flower made me think of you before that."

"Because it looks so cheerful?"

"Perhaps. That reminds me, how is your nephew? I've not seen him round here lately."

"He tells me he's fine, just really busy with work." Jerry made a mental note to mention her enquiry next time he spoke to Mike, in the hopes that might persuade him to take a break.

The conversation between Jerry the vicar vicar and Ellie the school teacher was unusual in that the height of the plants wasn't under discussion, but otherwise it was much like those going on elsewhere in Little Mallow. There was much praise for the most impressive specimens, and a fair amount of good natured banter about their size and whose was tallest.

Old Bert Grahame declared that his best plant was easily three times his own height.

"I reckon you're right, as I can look it full in the face!" his far taller friend, and champion veg growing rival, replied.

"I can't, Mr Grahame. It's much taller than me," Adam said, but as he was nine years old that was of doubtful consolation. Still it was kind of the boy to try, Jerry thought.

There had been a lot of kindness involved in the growing of the sunflowers. Those who didn't usually garden were lent pots and given compost and advice by those who did. People had watered the plants of rivals who went on holiday, not once carrying out their jokey threats of using sleeping pills to slow the rate of growth, or otherwise nobbling people's chances. They'd helped each other put up stout poles to tie gangly specimens to. When Mr Thomas, a retired maths lecturer, had gone out one windy night to fix his more securely he found a pyjama clad neighbour already doing the job, aided by Mary Milligan shining a powerful torch from her bedroom window.

As Jerry had hoped, when the competition to grow the tallest sunflower had first been proposed in the Kale and Snail and Anchor, the event had brought people together. Everything Jery saw and heard should be filling him with joy, but lately just the thought of those tall, sturdy, stems and bright flowers heading into the clouds was making him anxious.

It had started off very pleasantly in the Kale and Snail. Martin Blackman had made tremendous progress since the fire which had almost ruined him. As well as rebuilding the bar and kitchen, he'd created a micro brewery. His Solent Ramparts Ale had won a quite prestigious prize, and to celebrate he was selling the stuff at a very reasonable price. Jerry had been among those who'd partaken and had no quibble with the judges' decision. Perhaps ironically, the beer was very good at breaking down barriers and fairly soon the different groups of people had joined together.

After a while someone, Jerry forgot who, had suggested the whole village get involved in another competition. Tug o' war and cricket were suggested but not everyone could, or would want to, compete. Plus there was the question of finding suitable opposition. All the surrounding towns and villages had a much larger population from which to draw their teams, so Little Mallow would be at a disadvantage.

"Britain in Bloom?" Mary Milligan suggested. "That would be playing to our strengths as it were."

"Certainly we are blessed with some lovely gardens, but perhaps that's a little ambitious?" Jerry said.

"I suppose you're right, vicar."

It wasn't Jerry who suggested the tallest sunflower, but he did offer a space in the vicarage garden for anyone who'd like to compete but didn't have anywhere suitable in which to do so.

"Should everyone be given the same kind of seed, to make it fair?" Police Officer Trevor Harris asked.

"I'd like to get my own," Old Bert Grahame said.

"From the same place you get your vegetable seeds?" his friend asked.

"That's right," Old Bert agreed.

There were then the usual attempts to get Bert to divulge the source of the seeds with which he grew his massive leeks, enormous pumpkins, and gigantic onions. These were followed by the equally customary attempts to get Mary Milligan, who ran the Post Office, to give away the secret. It was somehow assumed that because Old Bert didn't hold much truck with modern technology he must pay for his purchases by postal order and Mary would know who they were made out to.

"A port and lemon might refresh my memory," she said. It did – after the first sip she recalled that her customers were entitled to confidentiality. "However, on the subject of seeds, I agree with Mr Grahame. It would be nice if everyone chose their own. That way we'd get a nice variety of different sunflowers."

"That's a lovely idea," declared Ellie Jenkins, which settled the matter.

It was eventually agreed that the entire rules were as follows – A. Entrants were to pay £5 into the fund to repair St Symeon's roof. B.

Tallest wins. Neither of these had been Jerry's suggestion, but he'd wholeheartedly agreed with both. The church roof fund needed all the help it could get, and what other criteria could possibly be the deciding factor in a tallest sunflower competition?

It was agreed there would be further meetings in the Kale and Snail to 'discuss strategies'. Mostly because the reverend was a sociable man who'd developed a taste for Solent Ramparts Ale, but also to satisfy his curiosity, Jerry had attended some of these. He was amused to discover how seriously some entrants appeared to be taking the competition – but perhaps appearances were deceptive?

Jerry didn't doubt that Bert Grahame was just one of those paying particular attention to the seed they bought. However he knew Mary Milligan and Ellie Jenkins were pooling resources in order to try selections in different colours with little consideration being given to obtaining excessive height.

Some sowed their seeds in pots, others direct in the ground. One method would apparently give them a good start, whereas the other avoided root disturbance later on. Some kept the seedlings in the warmth, or covered them with cloches, others felt this cosseting would 'force' tender growth which wouldn't be robust enough to reach colossal heights.

Everyone seemed to agree that feeding was important. Martin Blackman said he intended to use spent hops. "If they produce prizewinning beer, then maybe they'll also give me a prizewinning sunflower?"

"More likely it'll come up half cut!" said Honor Harlington-Smythe. "I'm going to use the well rotted manure from my horses."

"Don't forget you promised me some of that," Bert Grahame said.

"Buy me a drink and it'll be on your allotment first thing tomorrow," she said.

One of those who were growing their sunflowers at the vicarage claimed using racing pigeon manure, collected from his brother's birds, would make the plants grow quickly. Old Bert's explanation about nitrogen made that seem plausible, but from the way the man was happy to supply anyone who requested some, and mulched Jerry's roses without being asked, it seemed the main objective was simply to dispose of the stuff.

When Jerry mentioned that to the verger, he was told, "Very likely. I won't be using that myself. I've arranged to get some giraffe dung from Marwell Zoo. If anything will add extra height, it must be that!"

With anyone else Jerry would have assumed that was a joke, but with Arnold Stewart the verger he never could tell. Whatever he had used, the verger's plants flourished in their sunny patch of the vicarage garden. Unlike the legs of giraffes the plant stems were quite stout. Each were topped with several branches, each carrying a small, but perfectly formed, brilliant yellow flower.

"They look splendid," Jerry had told him earlier that morning.

"I must say I'm very pleased with them, despite them not being the tallest. I guess that's just as well. It might have been embarrassing if I won."

That had surprised Jerry. Arnold had many admirable qualities and a few odd traits. Excessive modesty didn't feature anywhere in the mix. He'd said nothing though, other than remarking he intended to stroll around the village and see how everyone else was doing.

The verger's comment had faded to nothing but a tiny niggle in Jerry's mind by the time he'd met Ellie Jenkins and been gently teased over his inability to hold a tune. It almost disappeared as Adam tried to console Old Bert Grahame over remarks made about the limited stature of both himself and his sunflower. The niggle returned and grew as he walked further and passed a fair number of very tall sunflower plants.

Many people had paid to enter the competition, and taken a lot of trouble to grow incredible specimens. Only one of those could be declared a winner – but who was going to decide? It suddenly struck him that the verger assumed it would be Jerry himself. Why? Jerry hadn't suggested the competition, nor that St Symeon's roof should benefit... but he had been present when those things were decided. Oh dear! Several people had bought him a pint during the various strategy meetings, joking it was a bribe. So sure was he that this was said in jest he'd not considered what it was they weren't really bribing him about. Now it seemed clear they too had thought he would be the judge. And the clincher – Jerry hadn't grown a sunflower himself. He'd fully intended to, but had absent-mindedly put his seed out for the birds and not got around to purchasing more.

"Uncle Jerry, what's wrong?" Mike asked.

"This tallest sunflower competition. Oh! Mike my boy, what a nice surprise! Can you stay for a while?"

"I can. I unexpectedly had a couple of days free so thought I'd pop down and see you and these sunflowers you've been telling me about. Your parishioners have put on a terrific show... I'd have thought you'd be delighted."

"I was until a short time ago when it dawned on me that I'm to be the one to decide the winner."

Mike grinned.

"You're looking just like Ellie Jenkins," Jerry remarked as he noticed his nephew's lip twitch and eyes sparkle.

"I think you mean I'd like to look at her!"

"I shall make sure you get an opportunity, just as soon as you've helped me get out of this mess."

"Sorry, I don't see how I can. I've hardly set foot in the village for months, but even I'd assumed that declaring the winner would be your privilege. I'm sure that's what all the entrants think."

"I suppose you're right," Jerry agreed.

"Don't worry," his nephew said. "It's not like a beautiful baby contest or best Victoria sponge where you risk offending everyone you don't pick. You just see which is tallest."

That was of some comfort. The decision wasn't to be made on personal preference or open to interpretation, but a matter of fact. It did however throw up another area of concern. "How on earth am I going to measure them?"

"That's a good question. As everything else seems to have been arranged in the Kale and Snail over a pint or two of Solent Ramparts, I suggest we head there to look for an answer."

"A very good idea!"

As Mike and Jerry walked towards the Kale and Snail, several villagers followed. All attempted to solve Jerry's problem.

"It's basic trigonometry," declared Mr Thomas, retired maths lecturer. "You just need to measure the shadow of the plant and the angle from the tip of the plant to the tip of the shadow. After that it's a simple calculation with sines, cosines and tangents."

"Easiest thing would be to cut them down," said Officer Trevor Harris into the silence which followed.

"Oh no, we can't do that!" Ellie declared.

"Definitely not," Mike said, backing her up.

"I admit it would be a shame when they're looking so good."

"Send young Adam up a ladder and have him drop down a string or something?" was another suggestion.

"I don't think..." said Trevor. The rest of his objection was drowned out by Adam's dad and his teacher Ellie, also saying it wasn't a wise idea.

Further suggestions included retractable metal tape measures being flicked skyward, and cloth tapes attached to very long sticks.

"We could call in the fire brigade," Mary Milligan said.

Ellie gave her a high five.

Mike scowled, then suggested an app on someone's mobile phone might do the trick. "Or maybe we could borrow one of those laser things estate agents have to measure rooms."

"What a clever idea!" Ellie said, and Mike cheered up again.

It was finally decided that everyone would measure however they liked, but wouldn't measure their own plants. Mike would be present at every measuring, to help if needed, and see fair play.

"In that case we'll have to get it done this weekend," Mike said.

Jerry didn't find it strange that although it seemed obvious that none of Ellie's plants were even half the size of many other contenders, Mike started with hers and took a considerable portion of Friday evening doing so.

Most of the other entrants opted to have their plants measured on Sunday, so as to give them a little more growing time. Jerry didn't mind. Those who wanted to attend his service would still have time to do so, it gave Mike a good excuse not to, and Jerry an even better reason to avoid any involvement in the process.

Over Sunday lunch, Jerry asked Mike how he was getting on.

"I may be visiting you more frequently from now on... but you weren't referring to Ellie Jenkins, were you?"

"I wasn't, but that doesn't mean I'm not pleased about... potential developments."

"I thought you might be. Hopefully everyone will be equally pleased when the winner of the competition is announced this evening."

"I have evensong at six," Jerry reminded his nephew.

"And I, and the measuring committee, will meet you outside St Symeon's afterwards."

"Good. Right. Excellent."

"Don't worry, Uncle Jerry. It will be fine, I promise you."

Jerry tried to follow this advice during his final service of the day. He was reasonably successful. As always the music lifted his spirits. Usually he had to content himself with listening, but the especially good attendance meant he could join in very softly himself without spoiling anyone else's enjoyment. He and the congregation emerged from the church and merged with those sunflower growers and measurers who'd not been in attendance.

Ellie Jenkins was the first to present her findings. "Three metres, two centimetres."

"Very impressive," Jerry said to Bert Grahame, whose plant it was.

Martin Blackman's plant was reported as being 82 inches and Mary Milligan's as nine feet eight.

"Excellent, excellent!" Jerry was mentally trying to divide by twelve and recall how many inches there were in a metre. Wasn't one about the same as a yard? That was three feet so...

"Vicar, did you hear me?" asked Honor Harlington-Smythe. "Nineteen two."

"Indeed I did." She had been present at evensong. In fact it was her forceful voice more than any other which had emboldened Jerry to sing himself. That made him feel very kindly towards her, so Jerry was pleased the measurement she gave was not for her own plant and he therefore didn't feel too guilty in questioning it.

"That seems a lot. Is it feet or metres?"

"Hands. As I told your nephew, if it's good enough for measuring horses..."

"Oh quite. Yes. Absolutely. Um are there any more?"

"Just one," Mike said. "We're just presenting the short list of..."

"Think you mean the tall list, lad," Bert Grahame quipped.

"That I do! Anyway, I noted the last one down." He produced a scrap of paper. "It says here, 'the length of me rule and the span of me hand, plus a brick and a half.'" He gave his uncle a wink.

Jerry thought for a moment. He was sure Mr Thomas could have done the necessary sums to work out which of the previous measurements was tallest, but from the eager look on his face he hadn't done so. Ellie Jenkins might also have managed the maths, had not her attention been distracted by Mike. Jerry certainly couldn't and he doubted anyone but the measurer himself understood that last one, which Mike had so carefully noted. The clever boy had given him a way out of making a decision.

"I declare it a draw!" he said. Then before anyone could express disappointment added, "I've just remembered, we never decided on a prize. How about I buy the winners a drink in the pub?

Everyone thought this was a good idea, and a few hours later they also decided that 'the longest runner bean' would be a good idea for next year's competition.

"As my nephew did such a good job today, I nominate him as the judge," Jerry said.

This was unanimously agreed by those present. Mike was not among them. Neither was Ellie Jenkins.

The End

About the author

Patsy Collins writes cosy crime and romance novels, several of them set in the Portsmouth area. She's also produced dozens of themed collections of twenty-four short stories. These include subjects such as crime, romance, gardening and family related tales, as well as some which are slightly spooky. Her books have an upbeat, feel-good tone. You can find details of them all at patsycollins.uk

'Fallen Angels - Alchemy or Artifice' by Vicky Fox

Introduction

Artists Robert McKinley, and Jack Seton are collaborating with Pre-Raphaelite painters Rossetti, Millais, and Holman Hunt in a rented country house near Guildford. It is 1848. Their models have been actors from a travelling theatre company under the management of a charismatic and sinister man called Jonathan Ede. They use extraordinary marionettes in the performances, allegedly ancient and valuable, and they have been stored in a cellar. In a storm, the artists move them to a chapel for safekeeping. One of the marionettes escapes and the acting troupe is now leaving to find it.

McKinley has fallen in love with the actress Teresa and is distraught at the prospect of losing her. Seton has been having an erotic affair with Lily who has encouraged him to believe that the marionettes are fallen angels. McKinley intends to interrogate one of the actors on the pretext of paying for the modelling work.

Extract

From Chapter 3 - Pitdown Hall

'I'm happy to settle up, both you and Teresa,' he said. 'Can you come with me now to my room where I have funds?'

They walked up to the Hall and then climbed the stairs to McKinley's attic room, and he went to the desk. He turned to the young man.

'What are they? The marionettes?'

Avery lowered his eyes. He was trapped and he wanted the money; McKinley was convinced he had no reason to lie.

He continued. 'There was one perched upon my roof last night. I saw it in the moonlight. It looked at me and I saw intelligence in its eyes. I saw it running through the streets of Portsmouth too.'

Avery blanched and crossed himself. He sat heavily in the chair and tried to decide how much to reveal.

After a while, he said, 'They belong to Mr Ede, he's had them for as long as I've been with the troupe, and he controls them with something called alchemy.'

'Yes, but are they demons?' asked McKinley, the other man shook his head. 'Fallen angels?' He shook his head again.

'Then it is as I thought: they are creatures he has made and given life to.'

Avery shrugged. 'I can't say what they are, but they can appear to change shape and so are useful as actors in a performance, and the audiences love them.'

'Are they free to leave?' asked McKinley.

'Of course not,' said Avery. 'People would be afraid of them. They're kept captive for their safety and the safety of the common man. We don't handle them without Mr Ede's say-so, and they must be kept locked up.'

'Prisoners, poor things,' said McKinley. He turned to Avery. 'And now one has escaped. What will it do? Where will it go?'

'It will try to go home I suppose.'

'Where is that?'

Avery shook his head. 'I don't know. Only Mr Ede knows that.'

He took the money owed to him and Teresa and went to leave. As he approached the door he turned and said, 'Teresa might know more; she's been with the company longer than me.'

'Teresa?' asked McKinley as a thought struck him. 'How long have you been with him?'

'Fifty-odd years,' said Avery with a sly smile. 'Since the reign of King George, the one that was mad.' Then he left.

McKinley reeled from the shock. If that was true, then Teresa was even older. It took a few seconds to understand what he had heard. Then he sat on the bed and tried to make sense of it.

He knew that in the sixteenth century, Queen Elizabeth had relied on the advice of an alchemist called John Dee, but that was 250 years ago. Could he have lived so long? Perhaps Jonathan Ede was another name for John Dee; the names were similar. It must mean that the philosopher's stone had been found, and life could be prolonged. For some reason, he had taken to the road and was wandering England with his group of actors and those creatures.

He could hear the other painters gathering downstairs and preparing to say goodbye to the actors and suddenly thought about Teresa. He must speak to her before they left. He ran down the stairs and started towards the company as it prepared to leave. From the side of the house, he heard his name being called, and Teresa was there in the shadows.

'I had to say goodbye,' she said, and he could think of no reply but took her in his arms and kissed her mouth. The smell of her skin was ecstasy to him. They clung to each other.

'Stay with me, I will marry you.'

'I cannot,' she said. 'But every October I visit a grave in a churchyard. We attend the Sloe Fair in Chichester, and Mr Ede lets me do that.'

'You mean Doctor Dee?'

She gasped. 'You can't tell anyone. Please, we are all in danger if you do. The world cannot know what exists here. We do no harm. Promise me you will say nothing.'

'Why won't you stay?'

'It's impossible. But I will meet you at the church of St Andrew's in the Oxmarket at noon four days before the fair starts. Please. I will explain then. You know one of them has escaped and he must be caught, or we shall all be at risk.'

'I love you,' he said. She kissed him again then pulled away and ran into the sunshine to join the troupe that was harnessing the horses and preparing to leave. He stood for a few minutes in the shadows until he had regained control of his emotions and then he sat on the steps of the Hall. He would not wave them off. There was a noise behind him and Seton ran out of the door.

'No, no, they cannot leave so soon,' he cried and ran to the lead horseman. 'Lily, where are you?' He went from wagon to wagon and tried to get into the covered vehicles. The men pulled him off and he flung himself at them to no avail. Each one of them was stronger than him.

'Where is she? She would not leave me by choice. She loves me. We love each other.'

A tall figure appeared from the last wagon and dragged Lily out. Her hands were bound in a cloth, and she had been beaten. Her clothes were torn and her hair wild and tangled. McKinley was shocked to see she had a swollen eye and bloody lip.

'Take her,' said Dee, 'if you still want her. But know that she's been used by every man in this company and many more besides.'

He released the cloth and pushed her from the wagon.

'Lily, what has he done to you? I'll kill him!'

'She has betrayed me and is of no further use. Take her if you must or let her die in a ditch like the animal she is.'

Millais, Rossetti, and Hunt ran forward as if to attack him, but the men of the troupe moved to meet them and Dee held up his hand, a movement that stopped them all. Seton carried Lily away from the departing wagons.

They left slowly. McKinley saw Mariel look back at him, but Teresa was focused on the way ahead. She knew to conceal her feelings, and he was sure he would find her again. Had she not told him when and where?

*

They helped Seton bring the injured woman into the house and took her to his room.

'He must not be allowed to get away with this,' said Millais as they returned downstairs.

'Who will prosecute him?' said McKinley. 'These women are his servants. He would be allowed to beat them if they were his family, and you saw how the other men roused themselves to protect him. No, he cannot be touched.'

He shuddered at the thought of both Teresa and Mariel being in the hands of that brute, but Teresa had survived a long time, and Mariel had made her own choice. He decided to question Lily as soon as she was fit to be interviewed. Seton was with her and was bathing her wounds. McKinley went and knocked on the door.

When Seton answered he carried a bloody cloth and came onto the landing, closing the door.

'She's resting. This morning, I told her she should not go back to him. That is how he knew I'd moved the angels. Sorry, the creatures. She didn't know what I'd done and when I told her this morning, she at once went to tell him. If one hadn't escaped, then all would be well.'

McKinley could see he was trying to make sense of it.

'Ede came at me with fury and accused me of taking it. I knew nothing about it, how could I? They were in the boxes, and I had wrapped them in canvas to protect them from prying eyes. The door was locked, it was as secure as the cellar but not as wet. I had thought to earn his thanks but when I told Lily she seemed shocked and left straight away. Why did he beat her?'

McKinley said, 'She showed them to you when they were singing didn't she? She took you down to them and let you believe they were angels?'

Seton nodded.

'So you naturally thought that a chapel would be a good place for them. But if they were formed of different matter, something that would detest a sacred space, then that would disturb them and as we know, one of them escaped.'

'Yes, yes. I see now.' He glanced back towards the darkened room. 'I must find some clothes for her. We will marry as soon as we can. Poor girl.' He opened the door.

As McKinley was leaving, the woman on the bed cried out and Seton rushed to her with soothing words. He left them and went to see what the other men were planning to do.

They were packing up their equipment.

'I'm sorry McKinley,' said Millais, 'but we've decided to return to London as soon as can be arranged. Cook and the maid have just arrived. We need to let them know we shall only be here for two more nights.'

'I'll speak to cook,' said McKinley. He would need to explain the relationship between Lily and Seton and perhaps she would suggest a place where they could buy clothes for her.

That evening dinner was a dismal affair. The painters had packed away their materials and Rossetti and Hunt had gone into Guildford to arrange transport to London. They would leave in two days, but they were keen to help as much as possible in the restoration of Pitdown Hall and Seton's care of Lily.

'Does he realise that marrying a woman like that will put him completely outside social circles? His family will disown him, and no one will engage his services. The Academy will cut him, and he will never receive any of the appointments that he could otherwise expect.' Millais thought he was making a foolish decision.

Rossetti expressed admiration for his romantic spirit.

'He's living up to the ideals of romantic love. Of course, it would be better if she died and then he could paint tragic portraits of her forever and write beautiful poetry.'

'Like Dante and his lost Beatrice,' said Hunt. 'I fear that would mean a trip to hell, but in the long run, I agree with you.'

McKinley listened to the debate and thought it ridiculous; he said nothing. He was afraid the woman upstairs might not be all she seemed. He did not know what effect the loss of Doctor Dee's alchemy might have on her when she was no longer part of his retinue. He feared it. How old was she really and would she age in front of their eyes? He half expected to hear a cry of horror from Seton as his lover grew old and withered in his arms.

He did not see Seton that night as cook had sent food up to his room. She had promised to find some dresses left behind by an earlier occupant of the house before it was rented out. Probably the old woman who had died here and left it to the distant family that now fought over it. He did not doubt that she would make Seton pay handsomely for the unwanted clothes of a dead woman.

There were no cries in the lengthening night, either of horror or of ecstasy. He did not look out of his window for creatures sitting on the roof in the moonlight. Sleep was a long time coming and when it came it was uneventful, seemingly dreamless and he woke relaxed. As memory returned so did the fear and horror of the last twenty-four hours. He must formulate a plan.

He decided that as soon as he could leave Seton, he would find the Prospero Company and he must carry out research on John Dee. If his suspicions were correct the man must be hundreds of years old. As well as his alchemical expertise and the loyalty of his troupe, whose lives had been prolonged beyond nature, he was knowledgeable and experienced. If McKinley intended to take him on, he would have to find his Achilles heel. The creatures in the boxes held the key.

Seton did not appear for breakfast that morning and the three younger men went out to sketch the house and surrounding countryside on their last day. Cook said she had taken breakfast to the couple and that the young woman's condition seemed to be improving.

'Did you see her?' he asked.

'No, I couldn't see round Mr Seton and the room was dark.'

She bustled away shaking her head.

McKinley decided he had to go and speak to his friend. He needed help and Lily was his best source of information if he was ever to find Mariel and Teresa. He knocked on the heavy oak door to Seton's bedroom. There was some whispering and then the door was unlocked by key and opened a few inches.

'How is she? Is there something I can do? Do you need the advice of a doctor?'

Seton opened the door a little wider and slipped out.

'I don't think a doctor would be any help.'

He was pale and tired, but he looked sheepish.

'She's changed Robert, virtually overnight. I've bathed and dressed the cuts she received when thrown from the wagon and I'm sure they'll heal. But she's so lethargic.' He looked downcast.

'She's had a beating, man, what do you expect? She's been cast out of her home and from her family. She's bound to be traumatised.'

Seton looked around miserably like a cornered animal.

McKinley realised he was having second thoughts about taking on a woman of her class and background. He closed the door. 'Do you still love her?'

Seton squirmed slightly and did not reply. It was clear that his lust had abated. Perhaps the glamour cast by Dee's alchemy had been instrumental in causing the passion, and now it had been removed. He had a fleeting doubt about his feelings for Teresa, but he had been nurturing them for many weeks, and they had not been satisfied in sin.

'Can I speak to her?' McKinley continued, even more curious to see the effect that the loss of alchemy might have on a woman who had lived goodness knew how long within its orbit.

'I promise I will not judge her, Seton, or you, but I need to ask some questions about the company and its origins.'

'She led me to believe they were angels. She didn't tell me they were demons or base things animated by demonic magic.'

He sounded like the mealy-mouthed parson he had almost become. McKinley wanted to punch him. He put a hand on his shoulder.

'Let me in and I'll see if I can help.'

They went into the dark bedroom. The wash basin was coloured with blood and McKinley told Seton to take it downstairs and bring up fresh water and towels if he could find them.

When he had gone, he cautiously drew aside the curtains, and the room was flooded with morning light. Lily lay on her stomach with the sheets wrapped around her. Her long hair was spread wide, and it was clear that Seton had been brushing it. Despite her condition, it had a lustrous sheen and a curl. She was awake and she slowly sat up with her back to him and began to collect it over her left shoulder. The sheet slipped down, and he saw she was naked and the bruises on her body were turning a mottled purple and red against her amber skin.

'Pass me the brush please,' she said and held out her left hand. She did not turn to look at him or try to tempt him and she seemed subdued. McKinley passed it over and she gathered her hair and started to plait it.

'I'm sorry for your situation Lily, but I must speak with you.'

'I think you've come to ask questions about John Dee. You know who he is, don't you?' She continued plaiting her hair.

'I guessed when the word alchemy was used, but I can't believe he could still be alive after all these years.'

'He discovered the secret of long life in 1605. He was fortunate to escape the purges of King James and to avoid punishment for his sorcery.'

'How did he escape?'

'By pretending to die of course. With the help of his daughter and the dismissive contempt that society holds for the old and poor. Nobody was interested at the time.'

'You've been with him for many years,' he said. It was a statement, and he knew the truth of it.

'Yes.'

He heard the smile in her voice, and she continued.

'He's drawn into his power those of us who were useful to him and kept us prisoners, like those poor creatures that are locked in the boxes.'

'What are they?'

'I don't know,' said Lily, and he knew she was lying. 'I wasn't really interested. He saved me, you see.'

'Saved you from what?'

She ignored his question.

'I loved the freedom of the open road and the power we had over audiences when we performed. It was the only time we really felt alive. It was the only time those creatures were allowed to be seen. He has them tightly in his thrall.'

'But not the one I saw on the roof,' said McKinley.

She turned sharply. He saw she was still bewitching despite her blackened eye. Her bruised, swollen mouth was more voluptuous than ever, like a fruit begging to be eaten. Her full, firm breasts bore as many bruises as the rest of her body, but her nipples were pert and dainty like purple flowers. She was not embarrassed. He sat next to her and collected a few loose strands of hair for her plait.

'You saw Gilgoreth?' she said.

'On the roof, Lily. What is it? It looked at me and there was intelligence.'

'He can fly you know,' she said.

'Is that how he escaped? Flew to the roof of the chapel and found some exit hole. How can a marionette fly?'

'They're the old ones. That's all I know about them. I don't know how long he's had them.'

She lied again but seemed regretful now she was parted from them, and because of that, or because he was kind, she began to weep.

McKinley felt sorry for her. He looked at her lowered head, she seemed vulnerable and feminine.

She said, 'They can heal you if you're ill.'

'Where will they go? I must follow them.'

'For Teresa?' she said turning her wet face up to him and appealing with her eyes. She had completed her long dark plait, and she twisted it around her neck like a scarf. Then she took his hand and lay down, on her back so she was naked in front of him. 'Don't go to her, stay with me. I'm free now and I'm tired of Seton. I'll give you pleasure you never knew was possible.'

She smiled and pulled back the sheets so he would be able to see her intimate parts and moved her hand down to caress herself as she made to open her legs. She tried to open them. She let go of him, moved both hands down to her thighs and tried to open them. They lay heavy and unresponsive. She did not cry out but opened her mouth, arched her back, and writhed on the bed.

Horrified by the sudden change, McKinley stood and went to the door.

'I'll fetch Seton.'

As he opened it, he heard a thud, and looking back he saw her clawing her way across the floor towards him, dragging her lower body like a serpent. Her pink mouth was open in a silent scream.

He ran down to the kitchen where Seton was looking at a black dress held up by the maid that cook had found for him. They were haggling over price.

'You must come. She's lost the use of her legs.'

They all dashed from the kitchen and stopped at the bottom of the stairs. At the top Lily was draped over the newel post. The exertion had brought more colour to her skin and the bruises were multicoloured, the patterning serpent-like all over her body. She saw them at the bottom of the stairs and reached out to them. Cook gasped in horror and the little maid screamed.

'No,' said McKinley as she slipped over the banister. Her heavy body fell, and the plait caught on the post. She only moved a little, then twisted round so they could see the staring sightless eyes and the protruding tongue. The maid fainted.

*

She hung like a carcase on a meat hook, twisting slightly, her eyes glassy and hands limp. The hair that had hanged her creaked slightly as she moved. There was no other sound until cook ran back to the kitchen.

The men were only then able to tear their eyes from the body and Seton dropped to his knees. McKinley thought with irritation that he was praying but he knelt over the unconscious maid. McKinley felt obliged to try and recover Lily's body. He leaned over the banister and wrapped his arms around her waist. She was hot to the touch and her skin soft and fragrant in a musky, animal way.

'For God's sake Seton, leave the girl and help me with this!'

He was able to swing her legs onto the banister and held them there. Cook appeared from the kitchen with a large knife and McKinley was alarmed until she mounted the stairs and cut the plait that had looped itself over the newel post. It took the strength of both men to bring the body onto the stairs. They looked at her naked form, her spread arms, and her closed legs.

'Don't stand there gawping!' said cook. 'Get the poor creature back into the bedroom and cover her up. I'll have to report this to the magistrate. Goodness knows what the owners will say when they hear of it.'

She accompanied them as they carried Lily back into the bedroom. She threw a sheet over her and said, 'Now out of here. I don't want any men near her. She'll have as much respect as we can give her in death.'

She shooed them out of the room, took the key, and locked the door.

The men made for the brandy that was kept in the sitting room.

After a few gulps, Seton said, 'She ... she told me she was a whore in London after the plague and the great fire when Dee found her. She was sick with the French pox and near to death. His alchemy saved her and gave her back the beauty she once had. She didn't know how old she was, but she had been sold as a child to men who liked little girls. Every day she drank a potion that Dee gave her to renew her beauty and keep the disease at bay.'

'Poor child,' said McKinley.

'What if I've got it? What if the whore passed the pox to me?'

Seton began to curse and sob.

McKinley slapped him hard.

'Stop it!' he said. Then more gently, 'You're in shock but you must pull yourself together and prepare to be questioned by the officers of the law. There will likely be a Coroner's inquest, and we know nothing about Lily. You can't tell them she's hundreds of years old. The Prospero Company has gone, leaving no trace of their whereabouts.'

He thought with foreboding that this looked like an abused woman beaten and murdered by her lover. Thank God the cook and maid had witnessed her accidental death. Cook seemed to be a sound person and would likely be known hereabouts. She will tell the truth and be believed.

Seton drank two more glasses of brandy and McKinley left him in a chair and went to find cook. She had sent the gardener to Guildford to tell the parish constable about the death. He would no doubt visit and examine the body then speak to the witnesses and the other occupants of the house. McKinley needed to inform the other artists as soon as possible and he found the gardener's boy talking to the maid in the scullery, trying to get details of the accident whilst pretending to care for her.

She was pale and wide-eyed. When she saw McKinley, she stood up shakily and he bade her sit. Then he told the boy to look around the grounds and tell the other residents that there had been an accident and a death and that they should return to the house at their earliest convenience.

He sat next to the maid.

'Tell me what you saw, please, in your own words.'

He wanted to ensure that she and cook had seen the same as he and Seton. There was no telling if the effect of alchemy might be different on men and women. They may have seen something else in Lily and her appearance.

'Cook told me I shouldn't say as what she weren't wearing no clothes, but she weren't, were she?'

'No, she was naked, having just got out of her bed and having been very ill in the night-time.' McKinley thought it right to bring the context to the fore. 'Go on.'

'Well, she were leaning on the banister at the landing. No clothes but her hair in a braid wrapped round her neck. Her legs looked funny.'

'Funny?'

'Like they were stuck together and painted red and blue and green. The ankles were bent back so she was resting on the tops of her feet. They looked uncomfortable.' The girl closed her eyes. 'Her face was terrible, all purple and white and I've never seen nothing like those eyes. Her mouth was open.'

'Did you hear her say anything?'

'No, but it was wide and red, filled with horror.' She was warming to the task now. 'She held out both arms and that made her slither over the banister. That's when I screamed. But her hair was caught on the post, and it jerked her back. She spun, then she hanged, moved a bit and she was dead. I don't remember any more. They say I fainted.'

'I'd say you remember very well. Thank you. That is how I remember it too.' McKinley was relieved that no alchemy had distorted his own eyes. 'That is exactly what you must say to the coroner's officer when he questions you. Leave nothing out and don't add anything that isn't true. Her nakedness is a matter of fact, ignore cook's prudishness.'

'But why was she all those colours?' asked the girl.

'She had been cruelly beaten by her previous master with the travelling theatre company. Mr Seton had been looking after her and he was fetching a dress for her when this terrible thing happened.'

'Oh yes, I was holding the dress when you came in. But sir, what happened to her legs?'

McKinley frowned at his recollection of the attempted seduction and her sudden paralysis and how he had fled. He should have stayed and looked after her; he was guilty of neglect.

'She discovered they were paralysed whilst I was talking to her, and I came to find Seton. It must have been because of the beating. If only she'd remained on the bed.... I am so sorry you had to see that.'

He heard voices as Millais and Rossetti returned, the gardener's boy and Holman Hunt were not far behind. He thanked the maid and took the men into the drawing room where Seton sat with his head in his hands. McKinley explained what had happened.

After a few moments, Hunt said, 'The scandal will ruin us. We must be kept out of this at all costs. I am planning to return to London tomorrow, that won't be delayed, surely?'

Millais looked sad but Rossetti was quite buoyant.

'It was never going to end well for that woman, she used her charms on us all didn't she? You're lucky to have escaped Seton. I suppose you're heartbroken.'

Seton looked up and smiled slyly.

'No, I think you're right, old man. I had a lucky escape,' he glanced at McKinley, 'and we have the cast iron witnesses of cook and the maid to ensure we are held blameless. Don't you think so McKinley?'

He had to agree despite being appalled at Seton's callousness and kept to himself the queer onset of paralysis and her reaction to it. From the moment of its discovery on the bed, when she was trying to seduce him, her voice had become as useless as her legs. Her screams were silent as she pursued him across the bedroom floor; and as she died.

'I don't suppose we could have a look at her,' suggested Rossetti. 'It'll take a while for the parish constable or whoever, to come up and we could make a few quick sketches. For art's sake.'

Seton replied, 'You'll have to ask cook. The door's locked and she has the key.'

They thought better of it.

About the author

Having a Fine Art and English Literature degree, Vicky Fox has always been an artist and only turned to writing during lockdown. In a world where real life provides as much sensation as a person can bear, she prefers to set her stories in an imaginative world based on real events. That way you can be sure of a happy ending but still have the experience of history.

Expect the occult in some form and plenty of folklore. Her books are available on Amazon. More information and artwork can be seen at www.vickyfox-alchemy.com

'The Perfect Fool' by Nick Morrish

Introduction

Unemployed journalist, Dillon Wright is held up by a group dressed as medieval knights engaged in digging up the Hatfield Tunnel. This bizarre encounter lands him a job investigating Britain's quirkiest cults, including Gnostics, prophets of doom and heretical nuns. Dillon has just escaped from a paranoid and heavily armed religious militia called The Defenders of the Faith. He expects them to be in hot pursuit but faces more immediate danger in the form of his accident-prone friend and housemate, Mark 'Sparks' Munro.

Extract

Chapter 17 Firestarter

Spring had been unseasonably warm, rousing woodland creatures from their hibernation several weeks early but now, with summer approaching, there was a cold snap. Sparks, whose mother had often complained that he had 'fish shop vinegar' running in his veins instead of blood, was not happy.

With Dillon away, Sparks was left wearing three jumpers and had no idea how to deal with the idiosyncratic central heating system.

It looked simple enough. There were only three buttons, a dial, and a limited number of permutations and combinations. How difficult could it be? But after an hour's fruitless fiddling, he was beginning to lose patience.

'Bloody archaic manual controls,' he complained to the empty air. 'This whole house needs a digital upgrade. If only we had Bluetooth, we'd be up and running in no time.'

He thumped the thermostat, but it failed to respond. As he squeezed his protesting arms into the sleeves of his winter jacket, he had an inspiration: last Christmas, Dillon had bought some coal for the open fire in the lounge but had been unable to get the fire going at all. The only rosy glow that Christmas had been from Dillon's cheeks, due to all the huffing and puffing.

Sparks, true to his name, was sure he knew how to start a fire. He turned his collar against the below-seasonal-average air and wandered out to the shed. All the essential items were there: a box of kerosene firelighters, several back issues of the Lincoln Free Press and Advertiser, the remains of the dead Christmas tree, and a large bag labelled,

'Smokeless Fuels, Industrial Grade Coke (approved for blast furnace use)'.

Sounds like good stuff, he thought, warmed already by fiery visions of molten steel. After a quick review of the principles of combustion, Sparks rolled up several entire newspapers and made a small paper mountain in the centre of the fireplace. He then piled a lopsided tepee of wood on top. In between the branches, he stuffed the entire box of evil-smelling firelighters. Finally, he went back to the shed for the coke, dragged the filthy bag inside, across the carpet, and proceeded to tip a good armful into the fireplace.

Once he was happy with the aesthetic look of his creation, Sparks struck an extra-long match and offered it up to the nearest exposed firelighter. To complete the combustion process, he blew hard into the grate and was pleased to see flames begin to flicker and dance over the paper as they consumed an article on pig farming with Dillon's name at the top. With the onset of hypothermia postponed, Sparks went back upstairs to fetch his laptop, so he could curl up next to the roaring fire while he read his emails.

Of course, the laptop was busy completing an update of some software he'd never used, and there was an unfinished game of solitaire running on his tablet. By the time he'd finished, it had become pleasantly warm in his room. There was even a faint wisp of smoke drifting under the door.

The fire must be properly roaring by now, he thought. Probably needs more oxygen. Perhaps I need to blow on it some more.

Sparks reached for the doorknob and that seemed quite warm as well. He pulled back the door. More smoke poured in, accompanied by small pieces of burning wallpaper. The carpet appeared to be melting, and the whole stairwell was like the inside of a factory chimney, with smoke and flames surging upwards and along the landing.

Sparks quickly slammed the door shut and reviewed the situation. He wondered if he might have used a few too many firelighters. There was no fire extinguisher in the house. All he had to hand was a half-empty Stingray water pistol and a small can of Red Bull. He manoeuvred the pile of used socks on the floor until it blocked the smoke seeping under the door, but the socks started to smoulder and the paint on the door began to blister.

Sparks wasn't one to give in easily, but it was time to abandon ship. He wrapped an old towel around his face and forced open the sash window. Without pausing to unplug the maze of wires, he ripped his precious laptop from its nest, tucked the tablet under his arm, and climbed out of the window. From there, it was a gentle slide down the outhouse roof, and a short drop to the garden below, where he landed, in a heap, next to the wheelie bin.

Once through the back gate, and with unaccustomed urgency, Sparks broke into a jog and made his way down the street, past the shops, past the bright red phone box, and into the taproom of The Queen in the Wall. Here, his cries of distress elicited immediate help in the form of a phone call to the fire brigade and an offer of free beer.

The excitement was all over by the time Dillon returned from Shropshire. The fire engine had done its work and departed, leaving the remains of his home smouldering in the watery, evening sun. A solitary policeman was there to greet him as Dillon approached the charred front door.

'Would you be Mr Wright?' the officer enquired in his best 'bad news' voice.

Dillon could only nod as he peered at the devastation through the window. 'Where's Sparks? Mark Munro, I mean. Is he all right?'

'Your friend is a little shocked. He was in the house when the fire started. But he's being well looked after.'

'Is he in hospital?'

'No, he refused to leave the pub. We thought it best to keep him there until some other arrangements can be made for you both.'

Dillon was more than a little shocked. He'd often joked about some cult or other burning his house down. If he'd genuinely thought it would happen, he'd have been a bit more careful in his choice of words. In his heart, he always believed that people were basically reasonable and could take a bit of a joke. Things like this shook his faith in human nature. 'The bastards. I didn't think they'd stoop to this. They could have killed Sparks.'

'I'm sorry, sir. Who are you referring to?'

'The Defenders of the Faith. It's hard to believe they'd be stupid enough to think they could get away with it.'

'Are you sure they were responsible, Mr Wright?'

'Well, who else could it be? You're not suggesting we burnt our own house down, are you?'

'Certainly not, sir, but could it not have been an accident?'

'If it was an accident, why does the place stink of kerosene?'

The police officer saw the logic of this. 'I have to say that I wasn't overly impressed with your friend's account of the incident, Mr Wright. However, I don't suppose he would be that foolish, now would he? He does claim to be some kind of engineer, after all.'

The officer escorted Dillon to The Queen in the Wall, where he found Sparks sitting in the back room of the pub, being ministered to by a couple of guardian angels, in the shape of Debbie the barmaid and PC Rosa Burkitt of the Lincoln constabulary. Despite the company, he was looking pretty miserable and, as Dillon entered, he began apologising profusely.

'Hey, I'm the one who should be sorry,' Dillon protested. 'I got you into this. I left you to face those maniacs on your own. There wasn't anything you could have done. I should have known they'd try something like this. Did you see them?'

'No, you see I went down the shed and...'

'They may have dropped some kind of incendiary device down the chimney,' the policewoman butted in. 'Part of the roof was destroyed and the fire seems to have started in the lounge. It could have been a petrol bomb or something more sophisticated. We're not sure yet.'

'I was feeling a bit cold, like, so I thought it'd be a good idea...'

'Are you OK, Sparks?' Dillon asked in a concerned tone.

'I'm feeling a bit woozy,' he offered, waving his fifth pint around for emphasis. 'But I managed to save my laptop and the iPad and a couple of me old LPs.' He patted the pathetic pile of belongings on the table in front of him and appeared to be about to burst into tears. Debbie clasped him even tighter to her ample bosom and PC Rosa Burkitt patted him on the head.

'Where are you both going to stay tonight?' PC Burkitt asked in a concerned voice.

'I'm open to offers,' suggested Sparks, optimistically.

'There's a spare cell at the station, or we could drive you over to the Salvation Army hostel.'

Dillon, having a rather more practical outlook, wandered into the busy lounge bar and scanned the crowd for a possible saviour. Soon, his patience was rewarded as the door opened to admit Steve Mathews, demon darts player and sole owner-occupier of a three-bedroom house on the nearby Carline Road. Dillon intercepted him as he approached the bar and offered to buy him a pint.

'What are you after?' asked Steve. 'I'm not buying you another pint. I've only popped in for a swift one.'

'Haven't you heard about the fire?'

'I heard the sirens. Are you telling me that was your house? Sparks been doing more rewiring?'

'Yeah, something like that. There was a problem with the heating. Burnt the place to the ground.' Dillon carefully omitted any mention of angry cults or arsonists, in case Steve considered such things to be infectious. 'We're temporarily homeless.'

'Shame. I'll buy a Big Issue off you.'

'We just need somewhere to stay for a couple of days,' Dillon pressed on.

'There are lots of hotels in Lincoln. It's very popular with tourists, you know.'

'And I'm going to be pretty broke for a while until the insurance comes through.'

'My heart bleeds.' Steve looked long and hard at Dillon as if calculating the risks. No one who'd seen how he and Sparks lived was ever likely to consider them ideal houseguests.

'One night and that's all. Just the two of you. No lasses, no pets, no smoke-damaged whatnots and you keep Sparks away from my electrics. If anyone even goes near the wine rack, you're both sleeping in the shed.'

'Thanks, Steve; I knew we could rely on you. You know what they say: a friend in need...'

'Is a pain in the arse. I know.'

It took a lot of persuasion to convince Sparks of the wisdom of this idea. He was especially unhappy at having to buy rounds all night to keep Steve sweet. However, the nice policewoman was long gone and no one else seemed keen to accommodate a couple of lightly charred ne'er-do-wells.

When Ed finally bade them a fond farewell with the toe of his boot, the three of them staggered along beside the castle walls, admiring the twinkling lights of the Tritton Road Trading Estate, far below.

Steve's house was spotless. Dillon and Sparks took their shoes off in the hall and hung around the lounge door, scared of contaminating the deep, cream carpet and the white leather chairs.

Dillon retreated to the kitchen to see about making a cuppa and Sparks followed. It was the tidiest kitchen they'd ever seen. Polished copper pans and gleaming steel utensils lined the walls. The worktops could have been used for surgery and there wasn't a cobweb to be seen anywhere. Sparks picked up the toaster, turned it upside down, and shook it. Not a single crumb fell out.

'Do you think he actually lives here?' whispered Dillon, filling the kettle from the multi-functional water dispenser.

'I dunno. I've seen cosier-looking show homes.'

From the hall came the low drone of the vacuum cleaner.

'It reminds me of that time when I had to work in the semiconductor clean room,' complained Sparks. 'I keep expecting someone to hand me a hairnet.'

'Shall I make a cuppa, Steve?' Dillon called out over the drone of the vacuum.

'Yeah, thanks. Use the blue cups, not the china, and be careful with the teapot: it was handcrafted in India.'

Steve reappeared shortly in his Marks and Spencer's carpet slippers and guided them into the safety of the dining room with its hardwearing parquet floor. Then he kindly fetched the biscuits, two each, laid out on matching plates.

'Do you get many visitors, Steve?' Dillon wanted to know.

'God, no! They do me head in, visitors. Takes forever to clean up afterwards.'

'Yeah, I know what you mean,' agreed Sparks, who was now regretting his wasted attempt to clean their house.

'Me folks come sometimes,' Steve added, not wanting to appear completely anti-social. 'And there's all the girls of course,' he added quickly. 'Lots of them, like. Well, a few, anyway. I prefer to play away from home, me. You know how it is.'

'Women make a lot of mess, don't they?'

'Too right. Handbags and shoes everywhere, your bathroom full of make-up and stuff. I can't be doing with it, me.'

'It's a very nice house, anyway, Steve,' declared Dillon, politely. 'You ought to invite the lads round sometime. We could have a great party here, loads of room.'

Steve looked horrified. 'No way! Absolutely no way! I had a barbecue here for the crowd from work once. They trampled all over the lawn, even though I put up signs about it, and then someone went and puked up in the rockery. They kept wanting to come inside for a piss and stuff. With their shoes on. Can you believe it? What a nightmare.'

'Well, it's good of you to put us up like this,' Dillon reiterated, though Steve's whining was starting to give him a headache.

'No problem, mate. When do you think you'll be leaving?'

'Oh, soon. Very soon, I'm sure.'

Dillon's phone buzzed. He held it gingerly up to his ear, expecting more bad news. Instead, there was the familiar voice of the brewery-owning Gnostic guru, Ralph Colemen.

'Hello, Dillon. I understand you have been experiencing some difficulties.'

'Ralph!' he exclaimed with some surprise. 'How the hell did you know?'

'I have my sources. Particularly amongst the connoisseurs of fine ales.'

Dillon bobbed and dipped his head in an effort to get better reception, but the crackle on the line merely turned into a whooping howl. He was genuinely pleased to hear from Coleman, but he was equally suspicious as to his motives.

'Did you know this was going to happen? Is it a sign?' Dillon wanted to know.

'If this was truly the work of the Defenders of the Faith, I am as surprised as you. This was never indicated. They may be dangerous, but for all their posturing, they rarely venture from their strongholds. Are you sure you haven't been upsetting anyone else, lately? A loan shark perhaps or an angry husband?'

'Definitely not!'

'Then I'm afraid we can come to no other conclusion. No good will come of this, of that you can be sure.'

'I thought you might say that. No good has come of it already. Our house has burnt down, my girlfriend's left me, and we're stuck here with Mr Ideal Home Exhibition.'

Their reluctant host could be heard in the kitchen, loading up the dishwasher.

'Got any bright ideas?' said Dillon.

'Indeed I have!' Coleman boomed down the phone. 'And I think, for once, that you will like this suggestion. Are you feeling adventurous?'

'Adventurous? Is that another way of saying heroic, or suicidal?' Dillon wondered.

'Not at all. No physical courage is required, though a certain mental resilience may prove necessary...Tell me, Dillon, have you ever heard of a group called the Wild Things?'

'Wow! I read about them in Prof Chowdary's book. I remember hearing some crazy stories about them when I was at college, but that was years ago. Are they still around?'

'Good cults never die, unless they commit mass suicide, of course,' Coleman corrected himself. 'Like our good selves, they are not quite what they once were. However, they still know how to enjoy life to the full. I can give you a telephone number. Once you have recovered sufficiently, why don't you call my good friend, Sheryl Keane?'

'What gives?' Sparks whispered in Dillon's other ear.

Dillon cupped his hand over the receiver. 'It's Ralph Coleman, the Gnostic bloke. He's fixed us up with somewhere to stay. Sounds pretty wild.'

'Nice one,' Sparks conceded. 'Steve will be pleased.'

18 Walk on the Wild Side

Breakfast at Steve's turned out to be Shredded Wheat and a mug of de-caff. By nine o'clock, Dillon and Sparks were in the Land Rover waving farewell to their host. Dillon parked the Land Rover in his usual spot next to the Central Library and the homeless and hungry duo went in search of a hearty breakfast. They wandered around the pedestrianised streets for a while past fast-food joints and generic coffee shops.

Eventually, they found a welcoming café at the top of the High Street and spent an enjoyable hour scoffing bacon butties, drinking tea and reading the papers.

The café had a crumbled copy of the previous day's The Sunday Echo, featuring a full-page article on the shenanigans in the Wyre Forest. It didn't mention Dillon's part in the proceedings, fortunately, but it did refer to Cult Report several times.

It was days such as these that justified Dillon's whole limited career in journalism, he felt. You could champion a worthy cause for years and never achieve anything, but occasionally, a chance word in the right place could start a story snowballing.

Dillon liked to think he wasn't a vindictive man, but anyone who could steal his girlfriend and make him get up at six in the morning deserved everything that was coming to them. Even if his writing never made a major contribution to world peace or the elimination of poverty, he could retire happy in the knowledge that he had introduced a little misery into the life of that odious little shit, Marcus Hardwick.

Feeling ready for the next challenge, Dillon decided to visit the Central Library for some essential research on the Wild Things.

'Forewarned is forearmed,' he explained to Sparks; adding hopefully, 'Two heads are better than one!'

'And too many cooks spoil the broth,' countered Sparks, heading for a nearby electronics superstore to check out replacements for his charred computer hardware.

The library was having a quiet Monday morning and Dolores was happy to scurry around looking for references to the Wild Things in her archives. After a little while, she came back with a couple of dog-eared books, a loose-leafed folder of newspaper cuttings, and a dusty DVD, which covered the subject in a fair amount of detail.

'It's a bit provocative, isn't it?' said Dillon, 'Calling yourself the Wild Things. Just asking for trouble.'

'Oh, that's not their proper name,' Dolores explained. 'Officially, they're called the Cult of Eternal Joy, though it's hard to imagine the Wild Things doing anything officially.'

'Interesting. They're the only cult I've come across so far that actually calls itself a cult. I like that.'

Dillon leafed through a couple of interviews with the group. It seemed that this perverse honesty came naturally to them.

With any luck, he would be able to tell the Wild Things' story without needing to burn up too much of his creative imagination.

The Wild Things was a nickname coined by a journalist who infiltrated the cult in the early eighties for a feature in Rolling Stone magazine. From the article, it sounded like he had a very wild time indeed. Unlike the majority of cults, who might have responded to this sort of intrusive behaviour with heavy threats and maybe a few burning crosses, the Wild Things refused to invite him to the next party. This, they seemed to consider, was sufficient punishment for any right-thinking individual.

'Here's something about Sheryl Keane, their founder,' said Dolores. 'She was a blues guitarist, but I don't think she was very successful. The music business is so very male-dominated, you know. She said she heard the voice of God speaking through her TV. I think she might have been taking drugs at the time.'

Dillon thought that was a near certainty. Judging by the size of Keane's book, kindly loaned to him by Delores, it must have been a long TV show. Either that or she made most of it up later on. Dillon had no intention of reading all his rambling scribblings, but the gist of his message was nothing out of the ordinary for a drug-addled cult leader. Apparently, the world would come to a sticky end sometime soon. Sheryl was advised not to worry too much about this, since a band of angels would appear at a suitable dramatic eleventh hour and carry the good guys bodily into Heaven. A heaven, by the way, which was a lot more earthly in its delights than the conventional biblical depiction.

Left behind would be all figures of authority, such as the police, government officials, and other likewise unpleasant characters. Right-minded people, such as Sheryl and her friends, were already "saved" and they could look forward to the big day with a clear conscience.

The new messiah saw this as an excuse to party on into the afterlife. With a philosophy like that, she didn't have too much trouble recruiting disciples. Soon the good times began to roll. Admittedly, God hadn't set up Sheryl with the music career she'd always wanted, but she quickly realised that religion was the next best thing. All the fun, without the need to toady up to slime-ball record company executives.

The Cult of Eternal Joy soon attracted a reputation for crazy parties and fast living. The police repeatedly raided the house in South London they were using as a base. Warrants were issued and Sheryl Keane decided it was time to move on. She still treasured childhood memories of a family vacation in Derbyshire. After a few false starts, God led his chosen few to the appropriately named village of Hope, where they purchased an old, abandoned station building and proceeded to turn it into a comfortable home from home.

Any antipathy that the local residents might have felt towards their new neighbours was soon dispelled by their exemplary behaviour, outside their own grounds anyway, not to mention the amount of money they spent in the local pubs. According to Dolores' records, their numbers had stayed pretty constant. One or two of the Wild Things got bored and wandered off every year, but there was a steady trickle of deranged and curious new members keen to take their place.

Dillon noticed that Dolores had turned away from her screen and was staring over her shoulder with a quizzical look on her face. He spun around and saw Sparks slouching towards them.

'Are you done researching yet? They chucked me out of Silicon World because they said I was being a smart arse. I was only trying to help. It's not my fault they employ a bunch of dimwits who don't know anything about computers. Or the outside world for that matter.'

Sparks was staring thoughtfully at Dolores. 'Your face looks familiar. I'm sure I've seen your profile somewhere. Heh, are you Guardian of Nineveh?'

'Yes, it's me! Call me Dolores. And you must be Divine Spark. Fancy seeing you here. I heard you were based in Lincoln, but I've never seen you in the library before.'

'Most people call me Sparks. I don't deal with hardcopy much.'

'Now come on,' said Dillon. 'You have to be kidding me. You two know each other?'

'Online,' explained Sparks. 'Not in the flesh, so to speak. We're Dataheads. "Information is Power", you know.'

'Well, that explains the geeky nicknames, I suppose. Divine Spark? Wait till the lads in The Queen hear about that.'

'Of course. Silly me. I should have realised!' exclaimed Dolores, fanning herself with her hands. 'That means Mr Wright is Sir Perceval, doesn't it?'

'Yeah, kind of,' admitted Sparks turning to Dillon. 'It's just a kind of online tag I gave you. No big deal.'

'It's because you are on a quest,' explained Dolores. 'Sir Perceval was the Grail Knight. The Perfect Knight.'

'Or the Perfect Fool,' said Sparks.

'Sir Perceval was a great warrior: matchless with lance and sword.'

'With zero control over his own destiny.'

'He was an innocent. Only the pure of heart could find the Holy Grail.'

'Ignorance is bliss, I suppose.'

'Oi!' interrupted Dillon. 'Are you talking about me, or this Perceval character?'

'Both,' said Dolores.

'Neither,' said Sparks. 'Can we go now,? I want to party on down with the Wild Things. Do you think we ought to bring a bottle?'

'By the sound of it,' said Dillon, 'that really won't be necessary.'

About the author

Writing under the pen name, Chris Blackwater, Nick Morrish has published two crime-thrillers, the first of which was shortlisted for the Crime Writers Association Debut Dagger Award. His latest novel is a madcap contemporary fantasy.

http://chrisblackwater.co.uk/

'Kissed to Death' by Gillian Fernandez Morton

Introduction

Five minutes is all it takes.

Five minutes in the wartime blackout. Five minutes that cast a long shadow. After war ends, little Kenny lives with his granny who can't find the words to explain where he has come from. He knows not to ask. His friend Gemma only knows her daddy from a framed picture on her mother's dresser. As the children grow up, they become aware of yawning gaps in their histories. They each meet a person offering shelter and warmth. But at what cost? What to do when a shelter becomes a cage? Who can dare to bite the hand that feeds?

Extract

Prologue

London 1944

Even now, when she shuts her eyes, she sees him.

It was the smell of him that had come first, even before she heard him emerging from behind that tree in the dark of the blackout. Beer, cigarettes and something else, something sour and animal-like. A smell which, after it was over, clung to her.

Yvonne had been walking across Southsea Common on her way home after the evening shift in the King's Arms. She'd liked the space after an evening of noise and crowds in the bar. These days the blackout never bothered her. The faint light from her torch was enough to see her feet. It was July so it wasn't cold, but the wind was suddenly quite strong.

No one was around to hear her cry out. Then she was sure he'd have hurt her more if she'd shouted out again, once he'd got her arms tight from behind and was wrenching her dress up, forcing her legs apart, shoving her face against the tree. The taste, the feel of eating bark. The sharpness of his knees against the back of her thighs.

A feeling of being ripped open, and the horror when he'd gone. She could hear his boots stumbling, running across the grass, leaving behind his smell. If she gets a waft of smells like that in the pub, or on the Underground of an evening, she has to stop herself from retching. Even now.

Somehow, she'd got home, got herself up the narrow stairs, trying to stifle the sobbing so Mum wouldn't hear. *Mum mustn't know*. First to the bathroom, dragging her damp flannel from its hook, scrabbling to turn on the tap to wet it, desperate to get clean, washing and washing, again and again, then to crawl into bed with her flannel between her thighs, horrified at the sight of the blood, and turned to put out the light. Trying not to cry with the pain, she'd called out to Mum to say she'd eaten something bad – didn't want anything – 'No, nothing, thank you!' Would she ever want to eat anything again? Or look at herself in a mirror?

*

When she missed her periods, Yvonne had wanted to get rid of it, hated to feel the alien presence of something growing, something left inside her by force. It wasn't long before Mum realised what was up. They'd argued and argued about getting rid of it, giving it away, but her mother was adamant that it wasn't the baby's fault. Any baby deserved love. And she could help Yvonne bring the poor little thing up, couldn't she? Her mum said they'd tell people Yvonne's secret "fiancé" had gone down with his ship in the Pacific. There were a lot of stories like that in wartime and people could think what they liked. But however many times Mum said "baby", Yvonne could only think of an "it".

After the boy's birth – again, a feeling of being ripped open – Yvonne had tried, she really had, but seeing it looking up at her, she knew it'd be seeing a piece of trash, a dirty piece of ... like she saw if she ever looked in the mirror. She knew she'd have to go away. Felt bad about taking the money from Mum's old jam jar on the mantelpiece, but she'd needed it for the train fare to London. Easy to lose yourself up there, people told her, to get some kind of a job in a bar or a club. And so it was all right, in a way, apart from the disgusting smell of beer and sweat from the men that made the bile rise up. And, of course, the dreadful raids, interrupting conversations or dreams. Mind you, she did find herself drifting off sometimes when it wasn't too busy. Would find herself back on the seafront. Before the war started and all the barbed wire blocked it off. Watching the waves with Mum in the old shelter, smelling the seaweed, hearing the seabirds squealing and quarrelling. Sitting out of the wind and staring at the boats on their way to the Isle of Wight. Her mother was always saying how one day they'd go on one of those big ferries for a treat. Have ice creams on Ryde Pier and even a donkey ride. But it never quite happened. Now, up in London, the Second Front was all people talked about. And of course, the doodlebugs. People often said, carelessly, 'if it's got your number', but you could see the fear that still flickered for a moment over some part of their face.

*

Back in her tiny London bedsit, Yvonne is carefully scraping out the last of her lipstick with an orange stick, then spitting onto the remaining scrap of mascara, getting herself ready for the evening shift at the pub. When she hears the approaching roar of a doodlebug, she thinks, everyone says you are OK if you can hear it but when the noise cuts out— In the sudden silence Yvonne catches a glimpse of her own terrified face in the mottled mirror, a second before the house fragments around her.

Crane Street, Southsea
1948

Elizabeth Siddons, hanging out the washing in the back yard, hears the plop of the soggy tennis ball on the wall of her terraced house. It's a comforting sound, reassuring her that her Gemma is playing outside with Kenny, the little chap from across the road who lives with his granny. They're still only four, but she's sure the children are safe enough out there. Hardly any cars. It's a dead end. Only ever the postman wobbling up on his bike, or the milk cart. How has that old tennis ball survived the drooling jaws of the street's dog? He appears as if by magic whenever the children are there, hitting the ball back and forth against the bricks.

The boy's not at the age yet to be asking questions. His granny has told Elizabeth how it worries her at night. Sarah says she'll explain when Kenny's old enough to understand. Not yet though. He won't have any memory of his mother, she says. Elizabeth would like to ask more about Yvonne's pregnancy but has never pushed. Growing up so close in this street the children are like brother and sister. At least Gemma's got a dad, even if she's seen precious little of him. Donald's still in uniform, away in Europe, dealing with the chaos in Hamburg's ruins. She guesses he'll turn up before long to get his demob suit for civvy street. Elizabeth isn't sure if that's something to look forward to or not. And he'll be like a complete stranger to Gemma.

Elizabeth realises she's been so caught up in her own thoughts that she's stopped pegging out the sheets. She reaches for the next damp, heavy whiteness to lift, spread and clip to the line. As the slight breeze lifts a few strands of hair off her face, she looks up, her attention drawn to the small biplane slowly making its way across the blue sky towards the sea. A good drying day, she thinks. Nothing to worry about now, but she's never lost the habit of listening out for a plane's engines, feeling a tiny sense of relief when it's gone on its way. Silly really, now the war's well over, but she knows she's not the only one. Those years here in Southsea left their mark on most people. After the Phoney War there was the shock at those first raids and then all the getting used to new things like the siren (Moaning Minnie everyone called it) that could turn your legs to jelly – running for the nearest shelter if you were out in a daylight raid – then the anxious hours waiting for the "raiders passed" signal. Nights huddled in the Anderson shelter, wondering what you'd find when you emerged, which house collapsed, which neighbour caught, either out in the street or under a falling wall or roof. People disappeared in so many ways. Everyone said they got used to it. 'If it's got your number on it...' they'd say, before complaining about the lack of soap or butter.

Elizabeth bends down to separate two red woollen socks embracing in her basket, and stretching back up, pegs them next to the last sheet before putting a hand to her spine, rubbing the stiffness as her thoughts drift. When someone just didn't come back...from abroad or just from the shops...or going off like Sarah's daughter, Yvonne, so soon after she'd had baby Kenny. All too hard to get one's head around. Someone you knew well enough to store a picture of them in your head, someone maybe you'd been impatient with the last time you'd seen them...and then nothing. Sometimes you'd see the telegram boy on his way to a door. Sometimes literally nothing. Like old Mrs Mortimer, the doctor's wife from the next street. Caught in a raid on her way home from the WVS. Nothing much left to put in the coffin, but no one said that out loud in front of the family. But her poor daughters...

Stepping back, Elizabeth checks her full washing line with relief. Hearing the tennis ball again, she wonders if the children will be off to the bombsite down the street where they often go when they aren't bat-and-balling on the outside wall. She's often watched them running in and out of the ruin's tall pink weeds, hiding from each other behind the half-walls as they play their endless games of make-believe. Sometimes children from the next street show up, all different shapes and sizes. Noise and sometimes tears, scraped knees, torn jumpers, and fallings-out. Nothing a bit of broken biscuit and a glass of lemonade in her kitchen won't put right. A wonderful playground now, but it had been someone's home. Still signs of it there, but broken and unoccupied, rosebay willowherb and buddleia half disguising the damage. Elizabeth shudders inwardly, for a moment picturing the young mother who didn't get to the shelter in time. Sarah thinks that when everyone else in the street heard the siren, poor hard-pressed, slightly deaf Hilda, must have been rushing to get dinner done before her kids got home from school. Probably with the Home Service on loud, so didn't hear the warning. Hilda's sad children live up north now with grandparents. Elizabeth is glad Gemma and Kenny won't be dwelling on the implications of the rain-stained scraps of floral wallpaper, which cling to one standing brick wall. But some things are hard to forget.

Elizabeth, with a small exhale of breath, pops the remaining pegs into their drawstring bag and, taking the handle of the empty basket, turns back towards the house

*

Sarah Crawley, hearing the thwack of the bat on the tennis ball and the children's laughter, looks from her upstairs window across the road and smiles as she repins her grey, untidy bun by feel. No use for mirrors at her age, and how many times has she put her hair up in her fifty-eight years? She loves to see them out there and as long as they are back in someone's kitchen by teatime doesn't fret.

It's Monday. Elizabeth will be hanging out the washing. She's a good friend. Brings her hot soup when she gets a bad cold, came in every day when she had that fall and couldn't even totter down to the Co-op. Sarah thinks it is time to cook Gemma's mum a fruit cake, she's been saving up a few currants for it. Elizabeth loves her cake. Sarah loves Elizabeth's smile. But she's uncomfortable when Elizabeth asks about poor Yvonne. Sarah's only told her the bare bones or, rather, the official version of what happened to her daughter. But this thought is a reminder. She needs to decide what to do – will have to explain it to Kenny in some way one day. Doesn't want to tell fibs but how can she possibly tell a little boy that kind of truth?

*

In the street, Kenny is brushing a dark fringe back from his damp forehead with one hand as he stands watching, resting his bat, as Gemma tries to reach the tennis ball before the dog gets his teeth around it. Gemma battles with the dog. 'Oh no, you don't, Champ. Give it here,' she says, and when she's retrieved the ball after a tussle, throws it back to Kenny, laughing and wiping her salivary hands on her shorts. He takes his best swipe to send it flying back to the red bricks. Gemma makes contact with her old tennis racket and sends it off again to hit the wall, but Kenny misses the shot and has to chase it down. With the soggy ball in one hand and his bat in the other, he stops to catch his breath for a second and hears the creak of his upstairs window over the road. Kenny watches his granny as she looks out and up at the sky. Momentarily he catches her frown, her downturned mouth, but then she's smiling down at them both, patting her coiled hair in that familiar way.

'Milk and biscuits in ten minutes, if anyone's interested,' she calls.

*

Kenny knows he was born in February 1944 because that's what Granny Sarah has told him. Of course, he doesn't remember that. No one remembers being born. Anyway, now he can recognise the big numbers on his birthday cards. Granny has shown him photographs, just one or two, of him when he was little. One is of him being held, wearing a little knitted bonnet, in a group of grown-ups outside the church in the next street. He doesn't recognise the grown-ups, except for Granny Sarah and Mrs Siddons, Gemma's mum, both smiling at the camera in smart hats and coats. The lady standing between them in the photograph isn't smiling. She looks as if she's seen something strange and worrying on the other side of the street. The other picture is of him lying in a big box, like a drawer maybe. He isn't smiling either. He has a thumb in his mouth.

Now, at four, he is allowed out (as long as he stays in their street) so he and Gemma, who is a bit taller than him even though two months younger, play ball on the wall of Gemma's house, or best of all, go down to the bombsite at the far end of the street. He and Gemma love its broken-brick corners, dark and smelly with mould, which lurk beneath tall, pink wild flowers. Places to hide, places to pretend you are a robber or a cop, Robin Hood or the Sheriff of Nottingham, or with the help of an old hat or some pigeon feathers, a cowboy or an Indian.

Kenny thinks there must be something secret about this place. Nobody talks about it, but he and Gemma spend many hours there. If he ever feels an unpleasant question rising in his head, he gets rid of it, hits it away with his bat, chases it off as he tussles with Champ. Life is too busy for questions.

*

Gemma doesn't recognise the man who walks up the path. He's limping a bit and is in a uniform. Elizabeth has told Gemma that her daddy is coming home. She can't remember who this is, even though her mum has told her that Daddy has met her once, but she was too young to remember. Gemma doesn't quite follow what Mum says, but it is something about far away serving his country and, since the war ended, helping people to get things straight after all the problems there.

It seems like her mum is pleased, and she has put on her special dress with a big rose pattern all over it, which she normally keeps for best, and her long fair hair looks all shiny. This makes her smell different from usual, not unpleasantly so, but it is unsettling. This man puts his arms around Elizabeth and then bends down to put a hand on Gemma's curls. The hand feels heavy and rather rough as it lands on her head.

At supper they sit round the kitchen table, three of them, instead of the usual two, so Gemma's chair is in a different position and she has lost her usual view of the room, which feels odd and a little disturbing. They eat a stew and some greens and a bowl of Gemma's favourite pudding, which she and Mum call fluffo, because of all the bubbles. It is made of evaporated milk and red, wobbly jelly cubes, which you have to tear apart (she loves that bit), before pouring on hot water so they can dissolve. Then it all has to be frothed up by the whisk. Elizabeth sometimes lets Gemma do a bit of the whisking. She likes the noise it makes when she turns the handle really fast and watches the tiny bubbles appear. You have to leave it then in the cool larder to set. It can be hard to wait.

Tonight's meal is either awkwardly silent, or the two grown-ups start to speak at the same time and then both laugh. Gemma just listens. The man is drinking something brown with a bit of froth on top from a glass. He has a moustache, and Gemma is fascinated by the tiny bit of froth that is clinging to his hairy upper lip. When Gemma gets up to go and get ready for bed, the man bends again to kiss her on the cheek and the smell of him is a bit sour. She thinks it is from what he was drinking. She feels uncertain. He looks like the man in the framed photograph on the sideboard who is called "your daddy". Except in some way she can't connect him to it.

*

Kenny's friend is usually in shorts and Aertex shirt, with grubby knees and tangles of fair curls. One day he and Granny are invited to a special tea at Mrs Siddons' house. Today, when Gemma answers the door, she looks all different in a floral frock with smocking across the front and a small white collar. Her hair is brushed almost straight and there is a gigantic, shiny pink bow pulling her hair off her face to one side. In the living room a large man sits in a chair near the window. He is in uniform. His thick, scratchy-looking jacket is brownish with lots of badges and pockets. Kenny scans the room for clues and notices the hat on a chair, sitting there like a snoozing cat. He is still staring at it when he hears Mrs Siddons say, 'Kenny, come over and say hello to Mr Siddons. This is Gemma's daddy.'

The man gets up and comes towards him, holding out a big hand. After a second or two staring at the hand, wondering about the thin white scar snaking its way through dark hairs, Kenny realises he is expected to touch it. When he tentatively moves his fingers towards the hand, the silence seems to go on forever, and then suddenly everyone is talking at once so Kenny can sink into the background. He doesn't think he has ever touched a man before. This is new. Hasn't ever seen Gemma in a frock before either, or with a hair ribbon. He feels a grumble in his head and a tightening in his belly. He moves back and takes Granny Sarah's hand, turns himself towards her to blot out the scene and hides his face in her skirt, which, comfortingly, always smells a bit of their little kitchen. Listening hard for clues, he hears that Mr Siddons is back from somewhere where there has been fighting. Kenny has heard about the war but doesn't understand. He's caught scraps of conversation between Granny and Gemma's mum, but they always stop when he comes into the room or the garden, or wherever they are talking. He isn't sure if that's because it isn't anything important, or it's something too dreadful for him to know about. Listening now, from behind Granny's skirt, he worries that his best friend has disappeared and been replaced by a stranger. Has Gemma gone forever? He feels an emptiness now in his head. And then a new feeling. He thinks he hates this man.

*

A few days later, Gemma knocks at his door, wearing her usual old shorts and shirt, her untidy curls no longer grasped by a hair ribbon.

'Hello, Kenny, it's only me. Don't look so surprised. Come on, it's not raining.'

They are soon off down the road with the tennis ball, and the old bats. 'My daddy's gone away again,' says Gemma, 'but look, Kenny, he bought me some sweets from the tuck shop before he went off. He said he'd have got more if they weren't still on the ration. Let's go down to our camp and eat them, like a picnic.'

Kenny feels as if the sun has come out.

About the author

As an educational psychotherapist, Gillian Morton used stories to help troubled children process their difficult life experiences. Her knowledge of the power of fiction to build understanding of real issues fires her own writing.

'Kissed to Death' is Gillian's second novel set in Portsmouth, where she grew up in the aftermath of World War Two. It follows 'Bombweed', the successful adaptation of her mother's wartime fiction. They are published by Silverwood Books, Bristol.

'Sometimes When I Sleep' by Helen Salsbury

Introduction

Influenced by Gothic literature, this coming-of-age story explores the intense relationships which form on the cusp between childhood and adulthood. It's likely to appeal to readers of Joanna Harris, Maggie O'Farrell and Holly Bourne.

For Harriet, Eden university is a chance to escape the shadows of a family tragedy and reinvent herself, even though she doesn't know exactly who she is or where she belongs. She's grown up hiding from curious eyes, and seeking refuge in the music of Dark Island, who appear to be the only ones who have words for her hidden traumas. Spurred by a promise from Dark Island that she's leaving the shadows, Harriet is convinced that university will be the place where all this changes. And yet, finding where she belongs is not easy. As the structures which have kept Harriet safe start to crumble, she comes to believe she has found a soulmate in the mysterious and compelling Iquis.

But neither girl is telling everything, perhaps not even to themselves.

Extract

Once

*"There was a princess,
dreamed from a drop of blood,
with skin white as snow,
with hair black as jet;
with her future carved in stone."*

From the album *Faerie Gothic,*
by Dark Island

One

Cumbria, 2004

'The University of Eden,' Harriet murmurs. Despite the tension in the car, the post-fight chasm between her and Dad, she has to say it out loud. Their car has been crawling over the vast shoulders of the Pennines for what's felt like hours, gradually climbing, gradually descending, and then finally this last turn in the road and there it is, nestled deep in the Eden Valley, all walls and buildings and green grass and well-trodden paths. 'Eden University.'

The taste of apples and the slither of serpents and the promise of something different, something better, something brighter. Harriet fights her seatbelt to crane forward; last time she'd only been a visitor, here for an interview. This time she belongs.

The road is narrow, twisting, and Dad has been hunched forward over the steering wheel for pretty much the entire journey: arms tense, shoulders bulked like a bull's.

She's kept a wary eye on him, unable to keep out of his way like she normally would after one of their fights. Now, she senses him turn his head briefly to look at her.

'You chose it for the name?' he says.

'No, I didn't! You *know* that.' She drums her trainers against the car floor, rakes a hand through her short hair.

It's not easy to let the anger, the resentment go. Never is.

She leans forwards, glares through the windscreen. In the distance, the sunlight is striking the white tops of Eden's residential halls creating a clean brilliance. And that lightens her mood.

There are no shadows there. It's a reinforcement of the Dark Island lyrics she'd heard for the first time this morning. "*You're leaving the shadows.*" That's what Medea had sung, that's what she keeps replaying in her head.

I'm leaving the shadows! She hugs the promise to herself, turning her head away to look through the side window so that Dad won't spot what she's thinking.

The free DVD of Dark Island's new song, "Bleeding for Strangers", had arrived in the post this morning, attached to the front of Harriet's goth mag. The timing was immaculate! Even though they were meant to be leaving straight after breakfast, Harriet hadn't been able to resist sneaking away to play it, using the excuse of ordering more library books for Mum to justify unpacking her laptop; only Dad had caught her watching it and been furious, their row so much more menacing for being conducted at low volume so that it didn't disturb Mum.

Harriet can still hear the words he'd snarled at her, can still hear the names he'd used for Dark Island. He'd called them "Ghouls". He'd called Medea a "grief harpy".

He'd not even tried to understand, even though she'd wanted him to; *really, really* wanted him to.

Dad clears his throat. 'You chose Eden for Dr Drake then?'

This is safe ground.

'Absolutely,' Harriet says. She hesitates, but the desire to get past their argument is strong. After all, how many chances has she got left to speak to him? She'd been looking forward to this journey, to having him to herself for once. 'She excites me every bit as much as she terrifies me.'

'Hmm.' It's a half laugh, encouraging.

'The way she grilled me at the interview,' she says, 'making it clear she's after brilliance, passion. She'll make me the best I can be. She'll teach me to build bridges.'

Then you'll be proud of me.

Again Dad clears his throat, an awkward sound. His fingers are clenched round the wheel, knuckles white. This journey can't be easy for him.

A sudden tightness in her chest, like someone has stuck her in a corset and pulled tight. She exhales rather noisily.

'You didn't have to choose civil engineering just because that's what I do,' Dad blurts. 'You're allowed to make your own choices.'

Harriet widens her eyes. Dad doesn't really do analysing stuff or heart-to-hearts.

'It's what I want,' she says.

And yet, she knows it's more complicated than that. It's what Stephen would have done. But to tell him this would bring them too close to what she fears is unsaid in every fight they have, the reason why they don't bounce back, the reason why no argument ever resolves things.

Dad and Stephen used to have epic rows. But there was never this awkward terrain of afterwards to negotiate, this smouldering half-life of anger, resentment, bitterness. Their rows always cleared the air, nothing was left unhurled, they'd emerge from their titanic clashes as bouncy as ever.

Bouncy. It's a funny word. Not one she'd use for Dad these days.

She looks out of the window into the distance, where the sharp peaks of the Lake District flirt with the blue sky. They are far less serious than the dour humps of the Pennines. It's another reminder that not everything has to be sullen-shouldered, hunched.

She immediately wants to visit them, and longs for her bike which just wouldn't fit into the car. She'll get it at Christmas when she goes home, bring it back on the train.

Dad thinks it will be easier for Mum to cope if Harriet doesn't keep coming and going, and Harriet hasn't argued with his conclusion, wasn't even sure she wanted to. She bites her lip, frowns. Will Mum be okay?

Surprisingly, what hits her is anger, rather than the usual guilt.

She clenches her fists and stares hard at the mountains until she's found a way to push it under, make like she never felt it. Impossible to feel anger with Mum, she'd have to be a monster to do that. And she's not. Doesn't want to be. Is intent on proving that she isn't.

She watches the mountains until the descent into the valley blocks them from view.

Nearly there! She rubs her palms on her jeans to dry them. She's nervous, inevitable perhaps, but it's all going to be okay.

I'm going to be a new person here. Not "the sister of the boy who—"

No. Not that. Not even *close*.

There's no one here from Harriet's school, no one here from her hockey team. It's the way she chose it. She's on her own, and she can make this hers. She can be whoever she wants to be.

Dad steers the car through the entrance to the walled campus and along its "fifteen miles an hour" roads, turns into a space in the car park, kills the ignition.

He stays sitting there, while the engine ticks. He looks tired, edgy, and there's a crease of frown just above his eyes. His hands are still locked to the steering wheel.

Finally, he lifts one hand. 'This is it. Genesis Hall.' He gestures at the square white building, with its splodge of red climbing plant. 'I'll start getting the boxes out while you pick up your room key.'

*

Every step is new; every face is new. Harriet does a fair bit of nervous smiling and saying, 'Hi'. Everyone's busy, either laden or returning empty-handed, like this group clattering down the stairs and past where the two of them are standing, checking Harriet's instructions on where to go.

'Top floor,' Dad says. 'Wouldn't you just know!'

Harriet hoists her hockey bag, with its clacking sticks, more securely onto her shoulder and shifts her grip on the huge box she is holding.

The stairs are currently clear; she gets a sudden impulse, acts on it.

'Race you,' she says.

It's an old game between them, but one they haven't played for a long time. He glances at her, a funny questioning look in his eyes, then says, 'You're on.'

They take the stairs two at a time, shoulder to shoulder. Harriet begins to edge ahead, then drops back. Dad is breathing hard, Harriet also, but more easily. She's been at hockey-club boot camp all summer, training and competing with the mixed seniors. Whereas Dad, who she always thinks of as fitter than her, has been stuck in the house when not at work. She slows her pace, lets him edge ahead. But then he too slows, and they arrive on the top floor together, shoulder to shoulder. A draw.

A couple of girls, who've been standing back waiting for them to arrive, grin at Harriet and Dad, then head off down the stairs. Another pulse of nervousness. She concentrates on finding her room, telling herself it will all be easier once she's on her own, unpacked, settled in. But she's really nervous now.

What if no one likes her?

But there's hockey, and there's class – no, she means *lectures.* There're lots of things she's good at. It occurs to her that she's never had to forge a new path. She's always been known – not always the way she wanted to be, but known nonetheless.

Her room is near the kitchen with just one other numbered door between her and it. There are voices in there, muffled by the thick door, people, floor mates.

Gulp! Not just yet. Got to unload first.

She unlocks her door and swings it open. The room is narrow, with bright yellow blinds concertinaed at the window, and a dense carpet, nubby and ungiving, under her feet.

Dad dumps his first load and heads back down the stairs, but Harriet lingers, assessing the room.

The desk is large and functional with deep shelves above it, just the place her Role Playing character sheets could go – her paladin, her trickster elf, her grenade-tossing princess – *if* she'd brought them. She'd wanted to, like a security blanket. Her gaming groups were another place she fitted, another place where she knew how to belong.

But there was no point in coming to university and doing *all* the things she'd done at home. And this was one sacrifice she was intent on making. If only because she'd always been convinced that Stephen would call her "sad" for holing up with the other gamers for hours and hours, for creating imaginary selves and existing in imaginary worlds, for wasting so much time inside. Impossible to think of Stephen sitting still for that long, letting his character do his fighting, his exploring, his roof-climbing for him. He just wouldn't!

She flushes, and turns to check out the pinboard on the wall. It's well used: covered in graffiti, embedded with drawing pins. She starts reading one of the jokes, *Why do lecturers...*, then breaks off as Dad comes through the door with her suitcase in one hand, her favourite pillow in the other.

'That's nearly it,' he says. 'You can pick up the rest as you see me off.'

Dropping the suitcase, he tosses the pillow onto the bed and walks to the sink. She watches as he splashes water over his face, then turns.

A thick stillness. There's nothing more to keep him. Unless –

'Do you want coffee before you go?'

He hesitates, then nods. 'You make it, while I give Mum a quick ring. Check she's all right.'

Mum!

The way she felt when I hugged her goodbye. So insubstantial – ghostlike in her fragility. As if I were already gone or as if Mum was. Nothing to hold.

Mum had stood just inside the open front door and Harriet could feel her longing to retreat.

'I just can't—' Mum had said.

Dad, pressing a hand briefly on Harriet's shoulder, had said, 'Get in the car,' and he'd turned back and taken Mum inside, and then they'd driven off.

Harriet hadn't looked back. So she doesn't know whether Mum was at the window waving, or whether the windows were as blank as usual.

And it's there again, that flicker of anger, resentment. She hefts the box of crockery and walks away.

'Coffee,' she says, as she leaves the room, takes the paces necessary to bring her to the kitchen, and pushes the door open.

*

She'd forgotten about the voices she'd heard, is unprepared for the two girls already occupying the kitchen, wants to walk out and walk back in, smile in place.

Fortunately, both girls are preoccupied, the nearest perched on a counter, texting, the other unpacking crockery into a cupboard. They have matching lengths of dandelion-blonde hair, falling across their shoulders and shimmering down their backs.

Harriet heads over to the kettle, which is steaming gently, and puts her box down. She rummages self-consciously.

'Is she back?' The girl texting doesn't look up.

'Nope, it's someone new,' the other says. 'Hi, I'm Jenna.' She closes the cupboard and smiles at Harriet, 'and that's Marcia. Are you moving in?'

Harriet nods, then hesitates. It's not just the hair, it's everything about them. Their cute, baby-doll T-shirts, immaculate jeans and most of all the similarity of their gestures.

'You're twins!'

'No shit, Sherlock.' Marcia's tone is more sarcastic than friendly.

Jenna laughs. A softer sound. 'Do you want a coffee? I was just about to—'

'I'm making one for Dad.' Harriet gestures with the mug which she's finally managed to unearth. It feels weird saying this, like she's caught between two worlds.

Just then he walks into the kitchen, pocketing his mobile.

'How is she?' Harriet asks in an undertone.

'Bearing up, but I ought to get back.'

'I know.' Her voice feels scratchy. She focusses hard on making his drink, splashing in plenty of milk so he can down it quickly. Tiny bubbles rise to the surface as she stirs.

A strike of heels.

'Iquis!' Marcia exclaims, sounding pleased.

It's an unusual name. Harriet passes the coffee to Dad, then turns.

And it's like Iquis has stepped out of one of Harriet's goth mags. She's framed in the doorway and her presence is huge. Maybe she's stopped there deliberately, for maximum impact.

She is vivid in her darkness: hair too blue-black to be natural, heavy-white face paint which contrasts sharply with the tar-black tyre-tracks round her eyes, a wide burgundy slash of mouth. A skinny ankh pierces her right eyebrow like an exclamation mark. She's high-fashion goth, very cutting edge, very modern.

Wow! Harriet wants to get to know her.

Harriet's never actually spent time with goths. She can't dance, freezes into red-faced immobility if she gets anywhere near a dance floor, so hanging out at Sheffield's one goth nightclub was always out of the question. She'd just have felt awkward, out of it.

It's surprising that Iquis is who Marcia has been waiting for; she is so opposite to the twins' shiny prettiness, so extreme. She's wearing a cropped PVC top and matching shorts from which squares of black mesh are suspended on tiny silver chains. Her skin gleams pearly pale through the fine mesh holes. She's tall.

Probably as tall as Dad. Glancing at him to compare, Harriet spots the forward jut of his chin. It's a bad sign. Given their recent fight over Dark Island, he's not going to be pleased about this girl.

But that's too bad. She grins at Iquis. *This* is her soulmate, the person she wants to spend time with, listen to music with – perhaps even share some of that black make-up with. *Anything* is possible.

Except that there's no response. Iquis regards her without expression. Her high cheekbones and razor slash of hair give her an arrogant look, a cold, detached appearance.

Harriet's grin lessens. Rebuffed, but determined not to show it, she gazes defiantly back into stormy grey-blue eyes.

And they get stuck like that. Neither giving an inch.

Harriet sees a brief, unforgiving snapshot of herself: her short hair, thin shoulders, too-big man's shirt and narrow face. Perhaps it's not surprising that Iquis doesn't recognise that Harriet belongs in her world. That she always has.

But she will, in time.

'Do you want to come to the bar with us, Iquis?' Marcia asks, but neither Harriet nor Iquis acknowledge this interjection.

Dad clatters his mug into the sink.

'Come on, Harriet, time I went.' He moves, steady and tanklike, towards the door, a collision waiting to happen.

'Okay, Granddad. Don't let me get in your way.' Iquis turns sideways to allow him room to brush past her. Although unsmiling, she seems amused. Harriet isn't. Dad is not fair game.

He says nothing, just moves to pass Iquis so that they are both in the doorway. Harriet can see the familiar anger working under his skin as he half-twists to look back.

Don't lose your temper, not here, she silently begs.

Iquis kisses him.

It's that sudden. That unexpected. He's there on the threshold, inches away from the goth girl's scantily clad skin, when she leans forwards and presses her lips into his. For a moment they are frozen like that, their mouths welded together, and then he throws himself off her. Hands slam into the wood of the door as he powers himself away and storms down the corridor, the muscles of his back bulging in outrage.

Impossible at first to react. The whole encounter seems unreal. Only the faint smudge of lipstick above Iquis's lip convinces Harriet it really happened. She starts forward: angry, disappointed.

'Why?'

Why did you do that? We could have been friends.

Iquis shrugs. There's the faintest hint of a smile playing at the corner of her mouth.

'Harriet! Are you coming?' Dad calls.

The girl winks at her and then with a sweeping gesture clears the doorway. The action disarms Harriet. She hesitates briefly, unsure what to do, then obeys her father. She will deal with Iquis later. As she sprints down the corridor, she is dimly aware of heavy perfume settling against her skin.

She catches up with Dad by the stairs. There's a burgundy smear, tangled in the black hairs of his hand, and a fresh awkwardness between them. Harriet is aware of a flicker of jealousy, as if Iquis has reached him, has touched him, in a way she herself has been unable to do. She pushes the thought away in disgust.

The incident makes it even more difficult to find a decent way to say goodbye. Dad puts the final suitcase on the pavement and Harriet piles her loaded rucksack on top. The car boot gapes empty, then he closes it. There's a brief hug – more awkward than usual – a quick exchange.

'I know you'll work hard,' he says, 'you always do.'

She nods an acknowledgement. 'Safe journey.' She thinks of the long drive ahead of him back across the Pennines to Sheffield and Mum. Strange to think of him "going south". Sheffield's always been the north until now. Cumbria has become the new north.

'You'll do well here,' he says. 'The Eden Valley's a good place.'

'I know.'

He hesitates, then adds. 'Stephen would have liked it.' He climbs quickly into the car, without waiting for her reply.

Two

*"Dark child we're losing you.
You're leaving the shadows,
Reaching for the light."*

Medea is singing the "Bleeding for Strangers" lyrics. Even though she's not visible in the video, Harriet pictures her: a white streak flashing from her forehead down through her long black hair, hooded eyes, the tightness of pain in her clenched stance. She always looks like that, tends to linger in the darkness at the back of the group. She's an alto, and her harsh saxophone voice is as rough and melancholy as ever.

'Grief harpy,' Dad had called her. Harriet is still simmering about that, can't help it. Doesn't he realise –

He doesn't, of course.

Medea sounds nothing like Mum, and yet Harriet has always made that connection, right from the first time she heard Dark Island, as if Medea can give voice to the things Mum doesn't say.

Harriet, cross-legged on this strangely firm bed with the laptop open in front of her, reaches forward and pauses the video.

This is where Dad had caught her, one stanza in, hardly started.

'This is not what you're meant to be doing!' His voice had been taut with anger.

She'd not appeased him the way sometimes she did, hadn't been able to, something angry in herself rising up to meet him.

'It's Dark Island,' she'd said, 'and it's just arrived. It's synchronicity. It's like a message.'

You see, Dad, she'd thought, *someone cares that I'm going away.*

She sucks in her breath.

Of course he hadn't understood anything. Dad had this huge hostility to Dark Island, an unreasoning dislike.

He'd told her to stop the DVD, and his voice had been flat, but the tell-tale muscle in his forearm twitched. He always thought with his arms.

'At the end of the song,' she'd said.

'NOW!'

She'd paused it, with the screen full of Circe's face – those china-blue eyes, that orange-red hair, that gothic-heroine look. 'You don't understand...'

'You're meant to be ordering Mum's books.'

'Yeah, I'll do that next. It's not exactly urgent, is it?' And then the *something* had driven her to utter the unsayable. 'It's not like she's going anywhere!'

His bicep had bulked as his fist clenched. She'd thought briefly that he was actually going to hit her – and some part of her had been pleased. As if, perhaps, it would explode once and for all that unrelenting tension. But he hadn't. Instead, he'd slammed the laptop shut and headed out of the house with it, saying he was going to lock it into the car boot, seeing as Harriet couldn't be trusted.

Left empty-handed in her room, aching to hear the rest of the song, Harriet had vowed that one of the first things she'd do when she got to uni was fire up the laptop and watch the whole video without interference, without anyone telling her to stop.

And now she can, as many times as she wants.

She restarts the video.

"*Dark child we're losing you.*
You're leaving the shadows,
Reaching for the light."

Circe, clad in a Victorian nightdress, is running to escape the other members of Dark

Island. She's trapped inside a turreted mansion and, as she flings herself through the maze-like passages, her blue eyes are wide with horror, her pouting red lips open wide in a scream which invades the music.

The running and the cornering is hypnotic, as repetitive as the drumbeat pound. The shaky hand-held footage makes Harriet's pulse race, and her headphones drive the sound deep into her mind.

Circe rounds the corner, slams to a halt and tries to back pedal. Sauron is there, wielding a bass guitar like a blood-axe, his face contorted.

*

'You're obsessed with that band.' Dad's words from the fight. Why can't she get them out of her head?

'It's about me,' she wants to tell him. 'It's like I'm Circe – we're both going away. And I just need to find out...'

What they have to tell me.

How it ends.

*

The house begins to split apart, walls cracking and rupturing, slabs of ceiling raining down. Dodging falling masonry, Circe breaks out of the house and hurls herself down the long, shadowed drive, until she slams to a halt, stopped by the vast, wrought-iron gates.

She yanks at them, but they are held shut by heavy chains, wound round and round and secured with a huge padlock. The sound of her struggle crashes and clanks into the music, as the gates sway and shudder. Then, with both hands – and superhuman strength – she breaks the padlock apart and hauls the chains through the gates, unwinding them, their heavy length clattering down into a heap at her feet.

"Dark child, when you're bleeding for strangers,
remember the darkness that gave you the light."

The gates swing open. As Circe steps through, the sun hits her flame-red locks and turns her into a blaze of light, burning her image into the screen until there is nothing but brightness, a magnesium glare which fills the entire screen.

Something about the brightness – the nothingness of the brightness – unsettles Harriet. It's too intense, it's like Circe is burning up in front of her.

She starts the video again, hoping for a different ending.

*

Later, when she sleeps, she dreams she is Circe.

The Victorian nightdress is tight across her shoulders, trapping her arms. It smells of oil and steel and when she looks down she's tightly wrapped in chains. They cross and recross her chest, pinning her arms and clanking. They hang heavy and cold. She feels shorter, like she's being dragged downwards, compressed.

What about the gates? Where are they? And Dark Island? Circe? She'll have the key. Or just... break the chain open with her hands.

The gates.

Yes – the gates. Harriet sees them now. Sees –

It's not Dark Island behind the gates. It's Mum and Dad; Stephen. Stephen's reaching out to her through the bars, his fingers curling to beckon, to summon.

Heavy with chains she shuffles towards him, dragging her way, obeying him, like she always does.

Then the shadows behind Stephen bulge and Stephen's best friend, Graham, steps forward. She can't meet his gaze. He's pushing forward to stand next to Stephen and she can't look into his face – but if she looks down she'll see his trainers, a gash like a wound across one instep.

And she'll know.

*

She wakes up.

She tells herself it was only a normal nightmare. Not the one – not the recurring one, which has haunted her for years, and been particularly bad in the last few weeks, so that she never wants to go to bed, because she's so terrified of encountering it.

Someone pushing her... forcing her to dig... the scratching sound of soil... the smell of decay... the opening earth...

No! Not that nightmare. But this one –

As bad. And somehow too close – As if the two nightmares are connected, and if she falls asleep now...

Well, she'd better not!

She pushes back the duvet, rolls out of bed. Nubby carpet, small room. Alien, really. Not yet comforting.

She doesn't dress, just puts on a sports-bra under her pyjamas, adds a fleece coat and trainers, then wends her way through the silent corridors and stairwells. On the ground floor she hears the faint sound of music travelling along the corridor and hesitates. There's someone else awake. But it would be impossible to knock on a stranger's door, with the fellowship of the night as her only excuse. And besides, she might say things she regretted, tell things which are better left in Sheffield, on the other side of the Pennines.

She shakes her head, continues towards the exit.

Outside she starts to run. She picks up speed rapidly, jettisoning her usual warm-up routine.

As she leaves the university behind, she loses the artificial light and runs on into darkness. Gradually her eyes adjust. There's a faint light from the crescent moon.

She's on a curving road, between walls. The night air hurtles towards her full of imagined obstacles. She speeds up, lowering her head to butt against them. She runs at this pace for some time, her body warming as her muscles relax.

The trees sneak up on her, solitary sentinels that draw closer together until they surround her, the tops of their branches reaching out to each other far above her head. They eat the light.

As the darkness thickens, her footsteps falter until she stops.

The wood creaks and whispers, and trapped pockets of cold air drift slowly towards her like ghosts. Her heart sounds uncomfortably loud.

'Who's there?' The words emerge without volume, disappear into the dark gaps between the trees as if swallowed by a great mouth. It increases her sense that there is some presence out there paying too much attention to her.

She swallows.

It's the dream. I ran away from it. But it's followed me.

The ground beneath her feet seems precarious. It could so easily crumble, give way, pitch her forward. She wonders if she is really awake. She presses her thumbnail into the palm of her hand, struggles to feel it and slowly backs onto safer ground.

For a moment she hears laughter – or thinks she does – then, just as her hand begins to throb in delayed reaction, the loud snap of a twig spins her around and she's running, faster than ever, back to the safety of the walled campus.

About the author

Helen Salsbury is the author of the gothic-tinged coming of age novel *Sometimes When I Sleep*, along with many published short stories. Her forthcoming novel, *The Worry Bottles*, explores how landscape and history shape us, and how we shape it. She is the founder of Pens of the Earth and the co-editor of their recent publication *Wild Seas, Wilder Cities*.

'Mute' by Richard Salsbury

Introduction

If Wes is such a quiet man – mute from birth, in fact – why does someone try to murder him one Friday night in the office toilet? Shaken, and dismissed by the police for reasons he doesn't understand, he goes on the run. But Keiran, his would-be killer and member of a survivalist cult, is not giving up, and tries to get to Wes through his wife, Alex. Though kept apart, Wes and Alex must find out what has happened and why. But when even the murderer's motives are unclear, who really holds the key to the truth?

Extract

Chapter 1

Some people had criticised Wes's blog for being too cynical, but the fact that a man had just tried to murder him in the office toilet validated everything he'd written in the past three years: *we're living in a madhouse*.

The weirdest thing was that he didn't feel more scared. He should be razor-edged, revved into the red. But years of martial arts training seemed to have dulled his reaction. He practised being assaulted every week, and now it had actually happened, his body was reacting like it was just another Monday evening. It was ready to settle into the familiar pattern: a curry from the Jewel of India on the way home and a night in front of the telly with Alex.

A bit more abject terror might have persuaded PC Bennett to take him seriously, instead of dumping Wes in an interview room and buggering off. He imagined Bennett at this very moment, sipping tea from a Hampshire Constabulary mug and chuckling to his colleagues from under that wispy attempt at a moustache, 'I've got a right one in room four.'

The interview room's walls were a flat grey, and a single energy-saving light bulb struggled to push the shadows back into the corners. It was designed for anonymity, for deniability. The only object of any note was the poster, showing a torso wearing a black T-shirt and leather jacket, the edges blurred to suggest motion. A fist at groin level gripped a flick knife. The caption: 'If it's longer than three inches, it's illegal.' Definitely one for the blog.

In fact, this whole episode was. In some cloistered part of Wes's mind he was already deciding how he was going to write this up when it was all over. Like a journalist who hid his delight in disaster, he was already thinking what a terrific story this was going to make. Astonishing that he could be so flippant after a murder attempt. If Wes himself couldn't take this seriously, why should they?

But it wasn't like he'd had the chance to express any of this. Where the hell had PC Bennett gone? Shouldn't he be taking his statement? Wes thought he'd made his situation – and its urgency – clear, but now the doubts began. Communication had never been his strong point. There was always room for people to misunderstand him, and the likelihood increased with those who were busy or impatient. His phone was out of his pocket and blinking to life before he remembered the bloody thing was still on the fritz. No way of texting Alex. Although, given their argument this morning, maybe speaking to him was not her top priority.

It was these two things – the argument with Alex and Bennett's non-appearance – that stirred up the first real feelings of fear. It was the old fear, reaching back into childhood and beyond, the fear of being misunderstood, of being ignored. Many times throughout his life he had thought this a thing of the past, something he had conquered. Every time it found a way to return.

The door opened explosively. Wes's feet jerked, and the chair screeched across the lino. A policeman stood there, framed by the door, but it wasn't Bennett. This man was tall and grey-haired, his face sheer as a cliff. The diamonds on his epaulettes marked him as someone with clout, unlike Bennett, who had seemed hesitant and distracted.

'Right,' the policeman boomed. He strode across the room, two quick paces, and took the chair opposite. 'My name is Inspector Selvidge. Let's hear what you've got to say, then.'

Blunt. To the point. Maybe that wasn't so bad. At least things were now moving. Wes fished out his notepad and a tiny mechanical pencil, and displayed the message he always wrote in thick felt-tip on the first page of any new notepad:

I'm Wes Henning.
I'm unable to speak
but I'm not deaf.

Selvidge's mouth moved, as if he were chewing gum. He took out a notepad and pen of his own.

'And your address?'

No, the bureaucratic niceties could come later. Wes flipped to the sheet on which he'd written his summary of events:

A man tried to kill me at work at about 18:00 today.

I've never seen him before.

Selvidge scanned the lines, then turned his eyes on Wes. He pursed his lips, tilted his head to one side. 'Okay, let's not jump the gun, Mr Henning. I need to ask you a couple of basic questions. The sooner we get past them, the sooner we can get to the nature of the incident. Is that acceptable?'

So, more delays, more faffing. It was a way, he supposed, for the police to deflect the frivolous claims, the weirdos, the nutters.

'So, if you could give me your address, Mr Henning.'

He bit his lip and wrote on the pad:

7 Oak Rd.

'Strathurst?'

Wes nodded. Yes, bloody Strathurst. Where else?

'And the incident occurred at your work, you say? Which is?'

J+H Web Design, Weaver's Down Business Park.

He paused, then added:

Strathurst.

Selvidge's pen moved across the surface of the paper, its whisper the only sound in an otherwise silent room. He took his time, as if the formation of the letters was more important than the information they conveyed.

'Very well. So, this man – how did he get into your office?'

It has an open reception area.

'With no staff?'

It's a small business.

'We deal with a lot of scuffles and altercations here, Mr Henning, especially on a Friday night. What makes you think this was something more serious?'

He said 'I'm going to kill you.'

'Well, that's very ... straightforward.' Selvidge placed the pen down on top of his pad. 'People are usually more cagey about murder.'

Christ. Surely even gallows humour had its limits.

'What sort of weapon did he use?'

None – bare hands.

'Bare hands? If he wanted to kill you, why would he just use his hands?'

How the hell should he know? Couldn't Selvidge get off his arse and *do* something? Wes put his hands flat on the table and tried to slow his breathing. This kind of thinking was not going to help. He broke eye contact with the policeman in an attempt to reel in his frustration. There was nothing else to look at but the poster – the actor holding a flick-knife and trying to look threatening. And now Wes thought about it, his attacker's lack of a weapon did seem strange. He had also passed up the opportunity for a surprise attack and waited until Wes was ready to defend himself. Why? Selvidge made him question his own story. And yet there was no doubting the ferocity of the attack.

A balaclava torn off to reveal a face he didn't recognise. Blows coming in – a jab, a roundhouse.

He saw Selvidge frown and realised he must have flinched.

'Would you like a glass of water, Mr Henning?'

Wes shook his head. He didn't want Selvidge leaving the room, getting diverted by a colleague who had mislaid the office stapler, and only coming back half an hour later when he remembered he'd left someone in interview room four.

'So, am I right in thinking this occurred in the reception area of your office?'

Well, no. Actually it occurred in the toilet cubicle, some of it on the toilet itself. Wes decided Selvidge didn't need to know this. He nodded again.

'Okay, so let's examine the question of motive. Why might someone want to murder you?'

Well, that was the crux of it. He could anticipate Selvidge's line of questioning because he'd already asked those same questions of himself, over and over. Could he put a name to any person he considered an enemy? No. Had anyone shown aggression to him recently? No. When was the last time he'd upset someone? Well, that would be Alex, this very morning. As he left the house, he could tell she wasn't happy – he'd never met anyone whose expression more accurately telegraphed their feelings – but he had gone anyway, the regret building up in him throughout the day. But there was no way he was going to volunteer this information to Selvidge. He knew how keen the police were to link murders to family members. It could only mean more dead ends, more wasting of time. Which left him with what? Although he had failed to dig up anything plausible in the last half hour, he had to offer something to divert Selvidge from his scepticism.

My blog?

'Your ... blog.'

It was a long shot. While *In Absurdia* was sardonic and biting, it was never aggressive. There were plenty of things in life worthy of scorn – corrupt politicians, vacuous celebrity culture, people's steadfast belief in idiocy – but Wes skewered them with a playful good humour. Granted, he had ruffled a few feathers on occasion, but he resisted the temptation to rant, and made sure his mocking never developed into a sustained personal attack. The blog was open for comments, giving anyone a chance to correct him or give their own perspective. Any arguments were short-lived. Or that's the way it seemed. Perhaps, somewhere away from the Neverland of the web, he'd kindled a seething resentment.

'You think a man tried to kill you because of something you wrote on the internet?'

Wes gestured that he needed time to think. The first thing that came to mind was his latest post:

Mrs Mute cracked a fingernail last week while hacking her way into the plastic clamshell containing her new headphones (she needs something to shut out my incessant jabbering). Why does packaging have to be like this? The answer came to me in a flash:

Company's desire for profit -> paranoia that products won't survive shipping -> vastly over-engineered packaging -> my wife's broken fingernail.

Another damning indictment of capitalism.

Mute

It was an observation capped off with a silly joke. Who could possibly be offended by this? People who designed packaging? Capitalists?
'Mr Henning?'
On the other hand, he *had* taken the piss out of people – the guy who took BT to court, claiming 'an unreliable broadband connection is suppressing my freedom of speech'; or the woman who had expunged a particular shade of red from her life because it had a wavelength of 666 nanometres and was therefore scientifically proven to be the colour

of the devil. These kind of stories were *In Absurdia's* bread and butter, and he expected a few people might be annoyed by them. But that was fine. Being told he was an arsehole every once in a while was part of the job, and something he was prepared to take on the chin. Being murdered in the khazi wasn't.

'Mr Henning?'

We're living in a madhouse. It was the first thing he'd written on the blog – both a fundamental belief and a mission statement. But in the last hour that sentence had taken on a very different meaning. It was the difference between watching a wrestling match from the sidelines and being pitched into the middle of it. Given that none of this made any sense to Wes, how was he supposed to rationalise it to anyone else?

'So, I'm assuming you can't think of a suspect.'

There were too many, that was the problem. Everyone looked like a suspect now, all of them equally improbable.

'I understand PC Jackson has examined you?'

Reluctant to be dragged away from his line of thought, but seeing no other option, Wes nodded. It had been a perfunctory check from a woman with all the bedside manner of a refrigerator. She had seemed unsurprised with his injuries – abrasions on the knuckles of both hands and the scalp above his left ear, some bruising on the chest. 'Been drinking?' she asked. 'Taken any drugs or medicines?' He shook his head. Her final comment to him – 'You'll be fine, dear' – had seemed more like a dismissal than a reassurance.

'You'll forgive me for saying so,' Selvidge said, 'but your injuries don't seem consistent with a potentially fatal incident.'

He was unarmed.

'And that's what I'm struggling with. If it was genuinely a murder attempt, he wasn't exactly trying very hard, was he?'

Oh, yes – easy to make light of it when you weren't on the end of those fists. Did Selvidge want the facts, or some idealised scenario that fit his idea of how things *should* have happened?

'You're afraid this man might have another go at you?'

Wes gestured that yes, of course he bloody was.

'All right, then,' Selvidge said. 'I have a proposal for you. We put you in one of our cells while we sort this out. We lock you in. No-one will be able to get to you there. You'll be absolutely safe.'

Wes had misheard him. He must have misheard him. The guy wanted to lock him in a tiny room, no bigger than a toilet cubicle, with no exits. Had no-one explained the purpose of the police to this man? The idea was to get the *criminal* behind bars.

Selvidge leaned back and folded his arms. 'Not so keen? Is that because it would prevent you from leaving the station as soon as you get bored?'

Wes shut his jaw once he became aware that it was hanging open.

'That's an impressive look of shock, Mr Henning, but let's review the facts, shall we? You claim that someone has tried to kill you, but (a) you have no evidence, (b) you can't suggest anyone who might have a motive, and (c) PC Jackson has singularly failed to find any knife wounds or bullet holes in you.'

So he had to be bleeding to death before they would take him seriously? Right. And presumably if the guy had attacked him with a knife less than three inches long, that wouldn't count either. Wes flipped over the page and wrote as fast as he could.

Selvidge didn't do him the courtesy of waiting. 'This is Strathurst, Mr Henning, not Syria. Do you really think we've got nothing better to do?'

I need your <u>help</u>.

When he looked up and held the page out to be read, Selvidge was leaning back, balancing the chair on its two rear legs. He glanced at the page, then back at Wes.

'Mr Henning, I have been absolutely fair with you. I've listened to what you have to say, just on the off-chance that it bears any resemblance to reality. Now I'm going to level with you. How many more times is this going to happen?'

They were confusing him with someone else. It was the only explanation. Wes had never been in this building before in his life. But as soon as he put pen to paper to explain, the chair thumped back down and Selvidge snatched his notepad away. Wes stifled his natural impulse: the curve of the arm into taan sau – palm face up, elbow in – that would deflect the policeman's arm away before he had the chance to grasp the pad. It was a reaction hard-wired into him from years of Wing Chun training, the sort of reaction that, less than an hour ago, had saved his life. It would do him no good here.

'Let's not waste any more time. This is your last chance to tell me the truth.'

Wes looked at the pad, caged under the officer's right hand, and his attitude set like cement. So this is what you got when you asked for protection – a silencing, a gagging. If you can't complain any more, there can't be any complaint. It was a shock, but not entirely a surprise. Part of him expected the world to be like this. Part of him said, 'See? I told you.'

'Very well,' Selvidge said. 'Because I'm a man of infinite compassion and kindness, I'm going to give you a choice: either you can go and tell your friends to stop this little game, or I can have you arrested for wasting police time.'

What friends? What game? Was Selvidge mixing up his cases, or was he jumping to conclusions without the faintest shred of evidence? It hardly mattered. Wes had run out of patience with this bullshit. He stood and jabbed a peremptory finger at his pad. Selvidge skimmed it across the table and Wes scooped it up. They glared at each other, and Wes had it in mind that he would make Selvidge break eye contact first, that he would win at least this small victory. But after a few seconds he began to feel like an idiot. The policeman was reclined in the chair, arms folded, perfectly still. You can't outstare geology. Wes turned, yanked at the door handle and headed for the exit.

From behind him he heard Selvidge's raised voice. 'Please do ask about the Independent Police Complaints Commission on your way out, Mr Henning.'

Back in the reception he saw PC Bennett leaning against the wall, arms folded, eyes tracking him as he strode to the door. Wes flipped him the middle finger and burst out into the night.

Chapter 2

Ten hours earlier

Alex made another attempt to get through to him during breakfast, while Wes was dipping a finger of toast into his boiled egg. The yolk, displaced from its bed of white, rose up and oozed down the side of the shell. She stood behind her chair, grasping its back and towering above him. He glanced up at her with the beginning of a frown.

Come on, girl, bite the bullet. 'I went to see Dr Clayton yesterday.'

He looked up. The frown deepened into a look of concern.

'No, no – nothing like that. I just asked her about … you know, what we were talking about.'

He shook his head slowly, and she suspected he was being deliberately obtuse. She put one hand on her belly and saw understanding creep across his face. He took two substantial bites out of his toast.

'I, uh ... I put your concerns to her.'

He focussed on his egg. Another plunge of the bread – another yellow uprising. Okay, perhaps she should have consulted him first, but it would only have made things more complicated.

He took the pencil and notepad out of his top pocket and wrote:

We discussed this last week.

Discussed, yes, but he didn't seriously believe they'd reached a conclusion, did he? Things had petered out after an hour and a half because they were both frustrated by the conversation, but that was in no way a conclusion.

'She said it was highly unlikely that any child of ours wouldn't be able to speak. Those were her exact words: highly unlikely.'

Speculation – she doesn't know.

'But what she said made complete sense. There's nothing physical about it, so genetically speaking there's little chance our child would inherit your ... problem.'

Even after three years together she still didn't feel right referring to it this way, although he'd assured her that words like 'disability', 'problem' and 'limitation' were all fine. The euphemistic approach was anathema to him. In one session with a psychologist he had lasted no more than ten minutes before walking out because the man kept describing him as 'speech free'. This was nothing to do with freedom – it was a hindrance, an obstacle to be tackled, every day.

Mental problems can be inherited too.

'I didn't mean that,' she said.

He shrugged.

'You know I didn't.'

Wes scraped out the egg white with his spoon and gulped it down.

'Don't be absurd, Wes. There's nothing wrong with you mentally, nothing at all.'

Evidently not true.

And technically, she supposed he was right. After years of examination doctors had found no evidence of a physical cause for his speechlessness. They concluded it was an inability to make the muscles of his vocal cords function, in the same way that most people never learn to move their toes independently. But that constituted a mental problem? Pure melodrama.

He was so difficult to argue with, all his communications so edited. With him, she missed the rapidity of normal conversation, because in amongst the jumble of words a truth could come out, something that might not otherwise have been spoken. It didn't have to be angry, just ... from the heart. And although it might be awkward in the short term, later you'd be glad of it. You'd move one step closer to agreement, or an acceptable compromise, or ... something. While Alex was quite capable of blurting things out – her overactive mind always ready to supply some random topic for discussion – Wes's thoughts always had the calm authority of the written word. She was sure it was her love of literature that lay at the root of the problem; his side of the argument always looked like Shakespeare next to her clumsy verbalisations. As soon as something was written down – even on the screen of a mobile phone or scrawled across the back of an Indian takeaway menu – it somehow acquired more firmness, more authority.

Out of nowhere, she was struck by a sudden desire for an onion bhajee – crispy on the outside, tender in the middle. What a perfect summary of where they stood: he was stalled on the very idea of having kids, while she was already jumping ahead to the food cravings.

And that's only half the problem.

'The other being that you wouldn't be able to talk to our child?'

He nodded.

'But I'd be happy to babble away enough for two. It would be no worse than being brought up by a single mother. I mean, Joanne copes fine with the twins, doesn't she?'

That's different.

'How?'

Kids emulate their parents.

'So our child would be a warm, lovely human being, just like their dad. I don't see the problem.'

A mistake: Wes had always been impervious to this facile kind of flattery. For him, praise was unearned without effort, without hardship.

You don't appreciate how I feel about my past.

It had been a long journey for him, to be sure, from bullied schoolboy to part-owner of a small business, but he'd conquered all problems in the end, leaving her in no doubt about his courage and persistence. So, having come this far, why this reluctance to take the next step with her?

Her own childhood had been considerably easier – a sun-drenched time in which her parents gave her boundless encouragement, love and indulgence. Having received such gifts, she longed to be the one to bestow them. Even if their baby was born without speech, they would be more prepared than Wes's parents had been. And if bullying became a problem, they could always opt for home schooling. For each of his fears, there was a solution. She saw the potential for joy and fulfilment where he saw only problems.

'Look, if we could remove these concerns of yours, then how would you feel about it?'

You can't do that.

'Of course we can. There's always a way.'

You can't just change reality to suit you.

'You make it sound like these problems are insurmountable. We're not trying to defy gravity, Wes. You didn't let a darned thing stop you when you were setting up the business. What's so different about this?'

Everything.

'I know what you're thinking – you might not put it on paper, but it's as clear as day to me. You think I'm being whimsical and flighty and ... you know I wouldn't be that way about something as important as this. The reason I gave up the tennis lessons and the accountancy course is that they weren't right for me. This – *this* – is the direction and purpose I've been looking for all along. There comes a time when a woman just *knows*. To hell with piecemeal secretarial work or trying to find a nice hobby. This is what I want. I've never been more sure of anything. What could be more important, more wonderful, than bringing a new person into the world? And now is the right time, Wes. Even if we started now, I'll be fifty-two before our child is out of their teens. Can you imagine that? Fifty-two!'

She was saying too much. He had taught her the art of the short sentence, the thoughtful pause, but still, sometimes she couldn't help it – the dam broke.

She finished her speech rather feebly. 'I don't think you know how I feel about this.'

He made a double-quote mark in the air. *Ditto*. When he wanted, his face could be as expressive as a silent movie star's. But in the last few moments it had hardened into blank neutrality, the doorway to his feelings closed. He was retreating, hiding behind his disability.

What if Wes shut down the discussion, said no, never, not under any circumstances? Was she pushing him towards this? And what would it mean for their relationship? She had not experienced doubts like these since the early days, when she had asked herself if it could really work with a man like this. Now they sprouted in her mind again, stretching out their tendrils like some virulent weed.

We've got very good reasons not to have kids.

'You mean *you* have.'

He stood up, and for a moment she really thought he'd lost his temper. He gulped down the last of his tea, tapped his watch and jerked a thumb over his shoulder, indicating that he was late, and he had to go. The clock on the wall took sides with Wes – no, he wouldn't make it in for nine o'clock, but given that he co-owned the company he could surely spare a few more minutes for her. It was an arbitrary deadline, another way of avoiding the issue. And meanwhile the hands on the clock kept turning, marking out the seconds, the hours, the years. She heard the scratch of his pencil and turned to see what he'd written.

We'll talk later.

Later. Always later. She wanted to discuss it now. He formed his index finger and thumb into a circle, raised his eyebrows. Okay? The clock told her how unrealistic she was being – you couldn't resolve an issue this big between breakfast and the drive to work. Why had she thought now was an appropriate time? Because it was an emotional decision rather than a rational one. She'd woken from a hazy, half-remembered dream in which her breasts were swollen, her belly gloriously full with new life, and Wes, without recognising the reason, had complimented her on managing to put on some weight. On waking, she was left feeling thin and hollow.

She followed him to the hallway, where he put on his shoes and coat. He gave her only a brief nod before he went out, closing the door behind him. So, no hug this morning.

Through the frosted glass of the front door she saw him dawdle on the step. He wasn't all that late, then. After a few seconds the letterbox opened. A folded sheet of notepaper drifted onto the doormat and his blurred outline diminished as he walked off to the car. She picked up the message and opened it.

I love you.

I love you.

I love you.

It wasn't fair. It wasn't fair because it was true, and she knew it, and it made her feel ungrateful.

She spent the day in a distracted, aimless mood, achieving nothing. It had been this way since she'd been made redundant from Spurling Wilcox, and the feeling would remain until she got another short-term job. There would be a period of interest when everything was fresh, but soon the work would become familiar, and then boring, with only the companionship of her colleagues to keep her going. Either she would leave in search of something new, or be culled through the vagaries of modern business.

She didn't just want a change, she needed it. And perhaps he did too, even if he wouldn't admit it. The problem was that her argument was with his perception of himself, with his inability to see Wes Henning as a good father. How do you go about changing someone's self-image?

There was no more contact from him throughout the day. She began to wonder, with increasing annoyance, whether he thought that he had made amends with that final note. As the sun set, and she realised she was watching her third episode of *Come Dine With Me* in a row, she lost her temper.

She stabbed the TV remote's off button and reached for her phone.

About the author

Richard Salsbury is a novelist and award-winning short story writer based in the south of England. His work has appeared in *Artificium*, *Flash Fiction Magazine*, *World Wide Writers*, *Portsmouth News*, the Fairlight Books website and on BBC Radio. He is an editor and website designer for environmental writing project *Pens of the Earth*. He also plays the guitar and brews his own beer. *Mute* is his debut novel.

'A Very Important Teapot' By Steve Sheppard

Introduction

A Very Important Teapot is the first of three Dawson and Lucy comedy spy thrillers, the others being *Bored to Death in the Baltics* and *Poor Table Manners*.

Saul Dawson, out of work and nearly out of money, has been offered a job by Alan Flannery, the bloke he thinks is his best friend. Flannery sends him to Australia and, once there, Dawson is instructed to head to a place called Yackandandah. He has no idea why and he also has no idea why he is then kidnapped by two goons working for gangster, Riley Bigg. He is even more nonplussed when he is rescued by Pat Bootle, the large, solicitor boyfriend of Rachel Whyte, the girl Dawson has designs on back in England. What's Bootle doing in Australia and who is he really? And why is Dawson also being trailed by the glamorous Lucy Smith, a girl he met once at a party who then disappeared as unexpectedly as she'd arrived?

Extract

In which Dawson gets a lesson in received pronunciation, and Pat rugby tackles a foreign woman

Even at the hectic pace Pat was pursuing it was another thirty minutes before the Mercedes entered the outskirts of Wagga Wagga, which turned out to be a much bigger place than Dawson had expected. There were a number of back streets disappearing into the dark on either side of the car and after a little while Pat turned down one of them, and then executed a number of further tight manoeuvres designed, Dawson supposed, to throw off any chasing Rambos or Chuckleses, before bringing the vehicle to a stop and extinguishing the lights and engine. He turned to Dawson. 'Now we'd better talk.'

'Here?' said Dawson. 'We're in Wagga Wagga, can't we find a pub or somewhere else a bit more comfortable? Possibly with an alcoholic drink within touching distance.'

'No, we can't. And it's pronounced Wogga Wogga.'

'They do well to keep that out of the guide books.'

Just then there was a knock on the driver's window, which made them both jump. Dawson, in particular, had had so many impossible things happen to him recently that he was beginning to feel he was in training for the Olympic high jump team. Even Pat looked momentarily disconcerted for the first time that evening but he wound the window down anyway. A handsome, middle-aged woman stood there, her face just discernible in the near-darkness.

'Can I help you?' asked Pat.

'I was about to ask you the same question,' replied the woman in a strange, lilty accent which Dawson couldn't place. Eastern European, possibly? Scandinavian? Not Aussie, anyway. 'Have you broken down, perhaps? Or are you doggers? It would not be the first time. I have had to call the police on many occasions.' Wow, thought Dawson. Do they have doggers in Australia? He'd thought it was just an English home counties thing, where frankly there wasn't much else to do of a midweek evening sometimes. The question though seemed to throw Pat, who had obviously not heard the term before.

'What are you talking about? Can you see a dog?'

There was something odd about the woman, Dawson thought. Where had she come from? There were no houses around, they seemed to be in some sort of industrial park. Personally he'd have gone for somewhere a bit closer to the centre of town, and once again the thought of a nice hotel with a cold beer on tap sprang to mind.

'Okay, let us forget that,' said the woman. Definitely Scandinavian, Norwegian perhaps. A long way from home but then she wasn't the only one. 'I think you had better be coming with me.'

'I don't think so,' replied Pat. 'We're quite all right. We don't need any help.'

'Oh, but I do need help. In fact, I think you can help me a lot,' said the woman, and suddenly there was a gun in her hand. Dawson was pleased that his instincts about her oddness had proved accurate but was less pleased about the gun.

'You're a bit less efficient at this escaping from the jaws of death thing than I thought, Pat,' remarked Dawson, who was by now resigned to whatever horrors were heading his way.

'You will please to shut up,' said the woman. 'Get out of the car. You are both coming with me.'

What with the appearance of the firearm together with his general latent cowardliness, Dawson was only too happy to comply with this instruction but apparently Pat was determined to be a little more obstinate.

'Listen, lady,' he said. 'I don't know who you think you are, or who you think we are, but I've called the police, so I suggest you pack up your little pop gun and scarper smartish.'

'Ah, you English, you are so, so funny,' said the woman, not noticeably laughing. 'You have not called the police.'

'How do you know?'

'Why would you have called the police? You are a criminal. You do not want the law to appear any more than I do. Now, do as I say and get out of the car.' She added, to Dawson's mind slightly unnecessarily, ' Or I will shoot you.'

Dawson got out of the passenger seat and moved around the front of the car. He was essentially quite cowardly, or at least he had always assumed he was, but then he had never before been in the sort of position he now found himself for the second time that evening. But then, as Pat opened the driver's door and started to heave himself out of the car, Dawson saw, almost subconsciously, that the woman's focus was concentrated on the elephantine figure of his companion. Equally subconsciously, he registered the darkness of the road they were in and suddenly he found himself sprinting off and half running, half leaping through some low shrubbery by the side of the road. The woman seemed to be caught rather unawares by this unexpected turn of events and it took her a second or two to turn and fire three quick shots in Dawson's general direction as he disappeared into what turned out to be an empty car park attached to a light industrial unit. Luckily, the direction of the shots was much more general than exact and none of them came close to hitting him. Dawson had never been hit by a bullet but he felt sure he'd know if it ever happened.

Pat was also surprised, which made three people out of three, but he was aware enough of the general sequence of events to allow him to launch his full seventeen stone at the woman in a rough facsimile of a rugby tackle. Rough or not, it had the desired effect and both of them went down in a heap, with the woman underneath. The gun went off again as the two of them landed, but the shot thwumped harmlessly into the side of the car.

Dawson heard the thwump, and also the similar but louder and thwumpier noise of the collision and landing. Then there was silence.

In which Chuckles and Rambo decide not to shoot each other, and Mr Big makes a telephone call

There had been a bit of a kerfuffle going on at the house outside Gundagai. Rambo was standing around, grunting incoherently and wondering what he could shoot at. He nearly shot at Chuckles as they appeared simultaneously around opposite sides of the house. Chuckles was yelling something about the car and someone he referred to as Mutt. Only Mr Big remained calm and unflustered. He was sitting in his black swivel chair and talking quietly on the phone to someone.

After a couple of minutes, he put the phone down, got up unhurriedly and walked out of the house. He was met at the front door by Rambo and Chuckles, the former continuing to make random grunting noises, the latter waving his arms around and still shouting about the car and Mutt.

'Be quiet, both of you,' said Mr Big. 'Go and get the other car.'

'But Mutt,' complained Chuckles. 'He's taken the pom with him.'

'Yes,' agreed Mr Big. 'It would appear so. It seems he may not be on our side after all, a bit of a surprise I'll admit, after two years. I guess I shouldn't have sent him to England.

Anyway, never mind, we'll be able to ask him in person soon. Now go and get the Range Rover.'

They did as they were told. Rambo in particular always did as he was told, as bitter experience had taught him on many occasions that going off on a limb without instruction was liable to end badly. Chuckles had slightly more ambition, but enjoyed the more violent aspects of his job specification so much that he wasn't sure if promotion up the food chain was really his thing. No, he was more than happy to take orders from the tall, bald man who'd picked him up from the backstreets of Melbourne three years ago as he stepped out of the prison gates after five years inside.

They were back with the Range Rover within ten minutes, Chuckles driving. Rambo had never got the hang of the automatic gearbox. And he'd never passed his driving test. The boss was quite keen that they shouldn't break such a small law. They had enough to do breaking big ones.

'Hey, boss,' said Chuckles. 'Where we going?'

'To meet my wife. I think she may have something for us. She's in Wagga Wagga, so let's be off.'

It took them less than an hour to reach Wagga Wagga and the house in Tolland that Mr Big liked to call home, although it had been someone else's home before he'd taken a liking to it. The house was in darkness, which seemed to surprise him. He nodded at Rambo. 'Check it out, Elsa should be here.' Rambo got out of the car, cradling his gun, and Mr Big punched a single digit on his phone and waited for a dialling tone which never came.

This was decidedly odd as he'd spoken to Elsa, his wife, from the house outside Gundagai and, by means of the tracking device clipped to the inside of the boot of the Mercedes, had been able to tell her exactly where Mutt and Dawson were headed, which coincidentally turned out to be Wagga Wagga. Like flies into a web, he'd thought. By now Elsa should have rounded up the escapees and brought them back to the house. He checked the tracker again and noted that the Merc was still stationary in the same place only a mile from where they were now. Rambo came back at this point and by a series of grunts and hand gestures managed to convey the information that the house was as empty as it appeared from outside.

There was nothing else for it. 'Rambo,' said Mr Big. 'You stay here and wait. Is your phone switched on?' Rambo grunted in the affirmative; after several years, Mr Big was able to accurately translate from the grunt 90% of the time. 'I'll let you know if you're needed. And if my wife turns up here, call me.'

'But boss,' said Rambo in a slightly alarmed voice.

'It's the green button. Just prod it and talk when I answer. Jesus Frederick Christ. Couldn't fart in a bottle,' he sighed. His staff recruitment had not always been spot on.

Chuckles got the Range Rover started and, following the beep from the tracker, it took them less than three minutes to arrive at where the Mercedes was. Except that the Mercedes wasn't. The beep though was of a volume that suggested that their eyes were deceiving them. They got out of the car and looked around in confusion.

'Get a torch,' snarled Mr Big, who was beginning to lose a proportion of his renowned sangfroid. Chuckles returned with a large flashlight, and within seconds they had located the tracking device lying forlornly in the gutter. Mr Big picked it up and looked at it. He called his wife's number again but got the same lack of response, so he tried Rambo who, surprisingly, managed to answer.

'Yeah?' Rambo muttered in the sort of tone that suggested he thought the phone might explode in his hand.

'Anything?' asked Mr Big.

'What?'

'Has Elsa showed up, you moron?'

'No boss.'

'Okay, we're coming back. Get inside the house and have another look round. A proper look. See you in five.'

'Five what, boss?' asked Rambo, but the line had gone dead.

6th Parallel

I was absolutely shattered following the flight back from Australia, so did as I was told like a good little girlie and went home to bed. I slept too, for about eight hours, but then woke up worried I was in the wrong country. I should still have been in Australia keeping an eye on Saul. Mr Napoleon-bloody-Flannery needed more than one "Lucy Smith" if he required me to be in both England and Australia at the same time. I'm more than confident about my resourcefulness, whatever he might say, but that was a stretch too far even for me.

When I got to the office just before two o'clock, it was almost empty. There was nothing unusual in that, Aardvark's manpower levels being lower than a tortoise's belly. Today, only our stalwart 55 years old Office Manager, Juliet, was there, sitting in her tiny office busy doing whatever it was she did. I didn't like to pry too closely. I actually have a theory that she is a spy sent from above to spy on the spies as it were. Conspiracy theories are ten a penny in this game.

Anyway, there was no sign of either Flannery or Rachel, so I girded my loins and approached Juliet. She had a disconcerting habit of peering at people over the top of her glasses and didn't disappoint in that respect now.

'Napoleon and Miss Whyte have gone to Croydon. To the offices of Franklin, Boasman & Bootle.' Well, I'm not stupid, I didn't think they'd gone shopping. 'I believe they have a warrant and presumably a small posse of police officers with them.'

'Thanks. Does he want me to join him?'

'I doubt if you have time before your plane leaves,' she replied, and suddenly, as if by magic, there was an air ticket in her hand.

'You're joking,' I said, grabbing the ticket, which clearly had the word Sydney printed on it. 'I've only just got back. Am I the only person working here?'

'One of very few, as you know. The office Christmas parties are always extremely disappointing.' That sounded like a joke, but the thought of flying back to Australia twenty-four hours after landing was not a joke. Meanwhile, Juliet was still talking. 'You'll need this too, I'm afraid,' and she picked up a passport from her desk.

'I've got one of those,' I said.

'Not with this name, Miss, er,' and she opened the passport, 'Morgan.' I took it from her. Apparently, I was now "Greta Morgan". I wondered how long that would last. "Lucy Smith" had managed to make it to about six months. Mind you, my new name had more of a ring to it than my old one, with a touch of foreign glamour thrown in. Well, the Greta was quite glamorous, the Morgan not so much. ScandiWelsh, I thought, perhaps I could come up with an accent to match.

I looked at the ticket again and saw that I was to be in steerage, as I had been for the flight back yesterday. Yesterday! The days of milk, honey and business class were a fading memory. And, wait a minute, what was this? Gatwick? I really had better get my skates on. 'Do you know what Napoleon wants me to do when I get to Sydney?' I asked Juliet. 'And please don't say "Await further instructions".'

'I do as a matter of fact, and frankly Miss Morgan, I'm surprised you have to ask. Not showing much of Napoleon's much vaunted resourcefulness are you?' But there was a smile behind the glasses. 'Yackandandah, my dear, get thee to Yackandandah. You never know, you might make the annual folk festival.' I quite like folk festivals, as it happens; in pre-intelligence days I'd been to a few and could erect a two man tent quicker than I could buy the beers to drink in it, and believe me, that's pretty damn quick. 'Seriously though, Mr Dawson should be there by now but we don't believe he is. You need to try to re-establish contact with him.'

'Actually, or visibly?'

'Visibly to start with. Then report back to Napoleon.'

'If he bothers to answer his phone.'

'If he doesn't, I will.'

In which Dawson emerges from the undergrowth, and makes good use of some jump leads

Dawson peered around the corner of the industrial unit where he was hiding to see if he could make out anything in the gloom across the car park. He couldn't. In fact, he could barely make out the line of bushes he had just scrambled through.

There was dead silence and he realised he couldn't really stay where he was all night. He faced a straight choice between trying to escape or retracing his steps to find out what was happening vis a vis Pat and the Scandinavian woman.

There was really no choice to be made. He edged out from behind the building and found himself actually and not metaphorically tiptoeing across the car park before realising how stupid that was and reverting to a normal, if cautious, walk. He reached the shrubbery and peered through it. He could make out the car now, and next to it there was another shape. Quite a large shape, but he couldn't work out what it was until the moon appeared from behind the cloud cover and he saw Pat, lying spread-eagled and motionless across the equally immobile form of the woman. A short distance away lay her gun so Dawson, gaining a measure of courage, pushed his way through the bushes and picked it up. It was the first gun he had ever handled and he didn't know whether it was still cocked or not. In fact, he didn't actually know what cocked meant, or whether it was an automatic and if it was, what that meant either, so he very gingerly placed it in his pocket, expecting all the time for it to go off and ruin his trousers, or something even more important to his life and wellbeing.

Having the gun in his possession gave him a bit more confidence, so he prodded Pat's recumbent form with his foot. Nothing happened so he pushed a bit harder and slowly, like some sort of giant jelly, Rachel's fat solicitor boyfriend slid off the Scandinavian woman and on to his back next to her. It was immediately apparent that Pat was bleeding quite heavily from a wound on his forehead, which would probably account for his unconsciousness, Dawson realised. He turned his attention to the woman, who was flat on her back and had clearly had the wind knocked out of her, and worse, by seventeen stones of chubby lawyer. Dawson suspected that this currently beneficial state of affairs was unlikely to last for long and so thought it best to tie her up as, awake, she'd shown all the signs of being quite dangerous.

That presented another problem, however, as he had nothing to hand with which to restrain her and even if he had, knots were yet another thing he knew very little about. He doubted that the method he used to tie his shoelaces would prove very effective in securing her when she came to. Dawson was starting to realise how unprepared he was for his new life of skulduggery.

He needed some rope, or at least some useful substitute for rope, and he didn't have time to go rummaging around in the dark in the rubbish bins at the back of the industrial units. Pat was a sizeable bloke and his collision with the woman had obviously been fairly cataclysmic, but even so she was probably not going to be unconscious for many more minutes and he pessimistically thought that even his current possession of her gun, bearing in mind he didn't really know how to use it, would be unlikely to tip the scales in his favour when she woke up.

He looked hurriedly around the inside of the Mercedes, but there was nothing remotely rope-like anywhere to be seen, even in the glove compartment. He found the button that popped the boot and moved round to the back of the car wondering whether there were likely to be any dead bodies in it and, if so, whether there would be room for Prat-the-Solicitor and himself as well. He took a deep breath and opened the lid, but the boot was empty. Wait a minute though, no it wasn't. Nestling in a dark rear corner was a plastic bag, and inside the bag was a set of jump leads.

They were better than nothing, so he scooped them up, ignoring the muffled clunk of something being dislodged and falling on the ground. He hurried back to where the woman was lying still asleep. With a bit of effort, he was able to roll her on to her front and he somehow managed to tie her wrists behind her with one of the jump leads. True, it was a bit too stretchy to make an ideal binding but when he'd finished, he was fairly confident that it would just about hold her for a while, so he repeated the manoeuvre with her feet and the second jump lead and stood up, feeling a little less useless.

At this point, there was a groan from the rather larger mound that was Pat. Dawson had no idea whether or not Pat was on his side but he was someone who had lately rescued him from the clutches of Rambo, Chuckles and Really Big and had not, yet, waved a gun in his face, so he at least had some credit in the bank. He found a large, hideous but clean, handkerchief in Pat's pocket in a shade of red that would help to hide the blood and held it firmly against the larger man's forehead as he helped him into a sitting position.

'Are you all right?' He realised it was fatuous question even as Pat's eyes blinked open and settled, glaring, on Dawson's face a few inches from his own.

'Fucking marvellous,' Pat said, slurring a bit. 'What happened?'

'Don't you remember?' The question rather worried Dawson. He hoped Pat hadn't lost his memory, as he'd quite like to ask him who he really was, what he was doing hanging out with villains in Australia and whether or not this meant the engagement to Rachel was off.

'I remember jumping on the hag with the gun. Where is she?'

'She's behind you, but don't worry, she's not going anywhere. And I wouldn't describe her as a hag. As gun-toting bitches go, she's quite good-looking.'

Pat had discovered that turning his head to look at the woman was not the wisest manoeuvre in his condition. He breathed deeply for a few seconds and dabbed thoughtfully at the wound on his head which, Dawson was pleased to see, looked less serious than it had appeared earlier.

'Can she breathe?' Pat asked.

'Does it matter?' Dawson was beginning to feel that they should be making tracks. Perhaps they could make an anonymous 999 call, or whatever the emergency number was in Australia, before disappearing in the Mercedes.

'Course it matters,' snapped Pat. 'Who is she? Where did she come from? How did she find us?'

'Coincidence?' asked Dawson in a small voice.

'I don't believe in coincidence but you're right all the same, we need to be getting out of here.'

Dawson didn't recall saying that out loud but he was in full agreement nevertheless.

'Help me get her into the car. And where's her gun?'

'Here,' said Dawson, pulling the weapon carefully between finger and thumb from his pocket and handing it over. Pat took hold of it with rather more confidence, then bent down and, without any apparent compunction, hit the woman over the back of the head with it before slipping it casually into his own capacious side pocket.

'Why did you do that? She was already unconscious.'

'Not for long. Come on, you take her feet. We'll stick her in the boot.'

'You mean, we're taking her with us?'

'Well, I'm not leaving her here. I need to ask her some questions and I'd have to shout very loud if she's here and we're a long way away from here. Which we need to be very soon, I suspect. She can't have come far, and where she's come from I imagine she'll have some mates wondering where she's got to. I should think they were expecting us back, either dead or nicely trussed up. Properly trussed up too, unlike the attempt you've made with her. I mean, jump leads? What were you trying to do, electrocute her?'

They managed with little difficulty to hoist the woman into the deep boot of the Mercedes. The keys were still in the ignition so Pat got behind the wheel and, hardly waiting for Dawson to slip in beside him, set off up the road. Soon, they were heading west out of Wagga and passing through a series of fast asleep little towns. After a while, just as they turned south onto the A39 at Jerilderie, there was a banging from the rear of the car.

'Ah ha,' said Pat, who judging by the small smile playing about his lips, appeared to have fully recovered his composure. 'We've got company. Time to find a place to talk, I think.'

About the author

Steve Sheppard has spent his whole life trying to discover the secret of how to become a fully-functioning adult. He has so far failed.

One thing he has learnt is that he ought to have tried writing a book forty years earlier than he did, although he also now realises that he should have become a celebrity first, as this would have made selling it much easier. He currently has three spy thrillers with laughs to his name, all published by Claret Press: **A Very Important Teapot** (2019) set in Australia, **Bored to Death in the Baltics** (2021), not set in Australia and **Poor Table Manners** (2024), which takes place in Cape Town. These feature a fairly hapless hero, Dawson, and a considerably less hapless heroine, Lucy, together with varied supporting casts, most of whom are not who they claim to be. The books have been read by approximately a million fewer people than Steve might have hoped. Despite this, a fourth title is on the cards.